MOUNTAIN MAN SCOUT

RUSTY STEEL

ASH LINGAM

I dedicate this book to the Mountain Men of times past.

1

RANDY STEEL

There was a time when Rusty wasn't a burly, bearded and menacing-looking mountain man. Back when he was a youth—he was also a braggart and a thief. Randy Steel was born and raised on the docks of St. Louis because his impoverished family couldn't feed their children. He did as many and robbed the local chicken coops and stole items off steamships. The docks were always chocked full of goods where a quick-minded thief could find the money to meet his daily needs.

One day when Randy was hiding in the shadows of a large barrel, he watched the passengers disembark from a sleek double-wheel paddleboat. He often spied on how the ships moved in and out of the harbor, using the port wheel to paddle forward while the starboard wheel paddled backward, turning the large vessel on its axis. He marveled at their maneuverability and speed along the treacherous waters of the Mississippi River.

His keen eye spied an easy target. A wealthy woman clutched her handbag as she unsteadily made her way down the gangplank. The harbor was awash with ships with massive paddle wheels churning up choppy waters, making the gangplank sway.

The little hoodlum waited until she was nearly to the end—then he saw her drop her purse. He shot out like a bolt of lightning as he sped past the stack of barrels. His legs pumped up and down as his heart hammered in his chest—he had the booty in sight. Just two more steps and he would be gone. Suddenly he was airborne—the ship's captain appeared from behind the barrels and snatched him up just as he reached for the bag. His feet continued to run even though they weren't touching the ground.

Capt. Samuel S. Bligh gripped him by the shoulders and gave him a shaking like he'd never imagined. His teeth chattered like on an icy winter's day. When he finally stopped and let him stand, he swayed from side to side as his head spun out of control. Randy wasn't ready when the backhand came—it knocked him off his feet, and he tumbled across the floating dock and into the water. The problem was Mr. Steel didn't know how to swim.

He slipped under the surface like a rock, then bobbed back up to the top again, his arms flailing as he grasped for breath. In his panic, he went under another time, then again and again. His eyes were spread wide in terror. He knew he was going to drown. Where did the captain come from? He had thought the coast was clear, but he was dangerously mistaken. He started to submerge again as he flapped his arms like he wanted to fly, but he disappeared under water yet again.

Captain Bligh immediately saw his dilemma—the boy was going to die by his very hands. He ran up and onto the ship and threw the drowning boy a lifesaver, then he reeled in the line until the young crook could climb into the boat. As he pushed himself over the gunnel, he rolled onto the deck and coughed up copious amounts of water. The ship's first mate pulled his tongue out of his throat, turned his head to one side, and pumped his lungs dry.

"Ya nearly killed 'im, Captain," First Mate Chuck Gordon huffed. "He's just a boy, for Pete's sake."

"I have a mind to throw you back into the water," the captain spat as he eyed the boy—still, he realized he'd overreacted. "If you wanna stay on my ship, when I speak and you don't do what I say, you're gonna get hurt. That's the way things work around here. And it don't stop until you do what I say. I'll just keep on hurtin' ya. If you steal again, you will stay where you stole—you'll be tossed into the river forthwith. I'll keep in mind that you don't know how to swim."

"Let the boy be, Captain," Chuck said to his boss of ten years. "Can't ya see he's homeless? Why, he's wearin' nothin' but rags. The Christian thing to do would be to give 'im a job and take 'im in."

"If he stays, he's your responsibility, Mr. Gordon," Bligh growled, yet concern etched his face. He hadn't intended to endanger the boy's life. He knew how hard living was for some on the St. Louis docks. "You can set 'im to scrubbin' the decks if ya want, but if I catch 'im stealin' again, in the water he goes, and this time he won't be fished out. Do you hear me, young man?"

Randy wiped the water from his face and nodded his head. He'd had the scare of his lifetime. He made a note to learn to swim as soon as possible so the same thing wouldn't happen again. Would they give him a job and let him stay? If the truth was known, the boy was plumb worn out from living on the streets. The captain stormed off and left the small crook and the seaman alone.

"Don't cha mind the captain, young fella," Chuck said. "He ain't nearly as hard as he acts. I was much like you when he hired me on this very ship. I was an ornery whippersnapper, and Captain Bligh saw it in his good graces to give me a job, and I've been with him ever since. Welcome aboard the *Dragon Queen*. What's your name, son?"

"Randy Steel. I was born not far from here. I grew up in the streets. I don't know why you wanna help me, mister, but I'm mighty obliged. I'm tired of not knowing where I'm gonna sleep at night. I've slept rough most of my life."

"I reckon I saw some of myself when you were drowning there beside the mooring. Everybody needs a second chance. The world is a hard place and doesn't suffer fools. You best keep that in mind."

"I'll work for my keep, sir," Randy said. "I ain't lazy. I can work as hard as most men."

"You better not be lazy because Captain Bligh has a whip he likes to use on the new men when they get out of line or shy from a chore. I doubt you want any of that."

That was something that Randy was going to suffer often because he couldn't manage to do anything quite right when the captain was around. When he messed up, he gave him a lash with his horse whip —just a single slap to the back of his neck. Not enough to seriously hurt the boy but enough to get his attention, although he always seemed to mess up again.

For the next thirty years, Randy Steel worked his way up the ladder on the waterways until he finally captained his own paddle-boat. He had filled out and grown long brown hair and a beard. At forty, he was already graying from long hours and endless days in the wheelhouse navigating the treacherous waters of the Missouri and Mississippi Rivers.

It was on a short stay back in their home in port in St. Louis when Randy was drinking with some of the crew in the Riverfront Saloon. Other sailors, soiled doves, and cowboys dotted the tavern. Kerosene lanterns hung from the ceiling above a hovering cloud of smoke. It was so noisy they had to shout to be heard.

A dozen Frenchmen sang drunkenly in the corner. Everyone in the tavern was deep into their whiskies. The cowboys had come from cattle drives and the sailors and officers from long voyages, and their thirst was unquenchable. Everyone was drunk—even Captain Steel.

Eventually, the Frenchmen approached the captain. Steel eyed the men suspiciously. He wasn't all that fond of Frenchmen, although they had the best relations with the Indians. Instead of trying to displace them, they traded with them and supplied them with metal tools. These items were valued with the Cheyenne and Crow, especially as they were friendlier with the trappers and hunters than were the Blackfeet and Pawnee Indians. That was back when all this land belonged to them. Even with the safety of the riverboat, they all knew they could only go so far up the Missouri River until it got too dangerous.

The Missouri was the longest river in the United States, stretching some 2,340 miles from the Rockies in the Eastern Centennial Mountains of southwestern Montana. It flowed south until it ran into the Mississippi just north of St. Louis. This made it the world's fourth-largest river system. The Missouri River had been a source of sustenance and transportation for twelve thousand years. The first white men to discover the furthest reaches of civilization arrived in the late 1700s.

This was a time when massive bison herds roamed the Plains. In 1803, the Louisiana Purchase made it American property. This deal nearly doubled the size of the United States.

To Jefferson's dismay, the spread of fear of an invasion from France traveled across the population. Napoleon even sent a military force to secure New Orleans. He eventually abandoned his plan to rebuild France's New World Empire. Luckily his attention was diverted to his imminent war with Great Britain. The Louisiana Purchase transpired, and the French sold the territory for $15 million or three cents an acre.

The Louisiana Purchase was negotiated between France and the United States without consulting any of the various Indians tribes who lived on the land and had not ceded the territory to any colonial power. This further opened the waterways toward the Rockies and passages beyond, but it also opened the dangers of traveling lands heavily populated with Indians. Some were hostile, and others were more friendly.

By this time, Captain Steel was aging and knew if he was to embark on a new adventure, he had to go soon, or he would be stuck carrying passengers and cargo up and down the riverways. The Frenchmen had an offer that sparked Steel's curiosity, and he couldn't help but consider their proposition.

"How about we pay you to take us as far up the Missouri River as you can? My name is Jean-Luc Vonore from the port city of Marseille. We have plenty of money for the journey. We want to hunt for cold winter beaver with the best pelts. That would mean we would have to dock the riverboat when the river freezes over and spend the winter. That will be the best time to trap coat beaver."

Captain Steel raked his fingers through his rust-colored beard and pondered the proposition. He owned his own ship and really could do what he wanted. He only had to hire another paddleboat to run his route for the duration of his current contract. His boat was old and had lasted much longer than the average four or five years. This was due to the skipper's skills as he avoided the snags and sandbanks that populated the river.

"What do you say, *mon ami,* Rusty Steel? *Excusez-moi, monsieur,* but your paddleboat has seen its better days. It may be her last adventure."

"What do you think, First Mate Gordon?" Captain Steel asked.

"The man has a point," Chuck replied. "The *Dragon Queen* has more patches than the sky does stars. What have we got to lose? You and I both have had a hankerin' to step ashore and explore the unknown for some time now. It can't be any worse than how we both lived as young men, now, can it?"

"Monsieur," Jean-Luc said, "we have plenty of funds from the French trapping companies in Europe, so if you are worried about it being worth your time—I can assure you that it will be a monetary bonanza for you."

"If'n y'all teach us to trap and track, it's a deal, by Jove," Randy Steel chuckled. He marveled at the prospect of changing the monotonous circle of routes he navigated over and over again.

Jean-Luc was very short, but his presence was immense. He had that charisma that some men possessed, knowing nothing wrong would ever happen to them, and their ventures would indeed work out. This confidence was contagious. The other five Frenchmen with Jean-Luc were all smiles. They had found the vessel they had been searching for. They were off on a special adventure to hunt and trap the best furs and the most dangerous animals—men and beasts—in the unchartered lands of the Americans.

The following morning, the Frenchmen were busy loading all sorts of equipment onto the paddleboat along with food stock, weapons, and plenty of lead balls and powder for their hunting plans. Stacks of wooden crates and dozens of barrels were hoisted by block and tackle, lifting the heavy cargo into the air, off the docks, and into the storage holds of the *Dragon Queen.* Sacks of coffee, flour, and cornmeal were loaded beside bails of tobacco. Then came the assortment of steel implements. There appeared to be enough to supply an army. These goods were accompanied by box after box of fancy Italian beads.

"What are the beads for, Jean-Luc?" Chuck asked. "They be mighty pretty, but wouldn't the space be better used for tools and food? Where's all the traps?"

"The traps are stored in the heavy long crates." The small Frenchman smiled. "The only thing the Native Americans like more than blankets and steel knives are colored beads. I joke you not, *mon ami*. They are like gold for the Indians."

Once Chuck had the captain alone for a moment, he expressed his concern about the pending voyage. He was just as excited as the captain, but he wanted to discuss the nuts and bolts of the plan.

"Don't you think we be heading out a little late in the season?" First Mate Gordon asked the captain. "We want to get as far as we can upriver before we get frozen in. That and we're gonna have to make sure we don't get stranded in the ice where we won't have a good winter supply of firewood to keep us warm."

"We have a good month or so before any chance of the first river freeze until we get up into Montana. Most of the rainy season is passed by the second or third of October. I was working on my charts for two years with something similar in mind. I'm tired of transporting unfriendly folks up and down the river. I reckon it was time for a change a couple of years ago."

"Did you hear that Frenchman call you Rusty?" Chuck said. "It sort of fits ya, boss. You know, with your beard going rusty colored and all. I reckon if'n I plan on going on such an expedition, I'm gonna have to get me a nickname too like all them folks that travel west."

"I reckon some change their names to escape something they be running away from," Captain Steel said. "Maybe even the law. Others may be running from themselves. We be running from a monotonous job. I reckon this will be our last chance to latch onto some excitement, and I don't plan to pass it up. If Jean-Luc wants to call me Rusty, that's fine with me."

2

DEPARTURE

The old riverboat decks were stocked to the ceiling, and the holds were bursting at the brims. When Jean-Luc said they intended to bring all the necessary provisions, he wasn't joking. They had included things that Captain Steel couldn't even identify. Several freed slaves joined the party of Frenchmen loading the ship. Finally, the animals were herded into the stables, and the chicken hatches were stored below. Jean-Luc demanded he had *les oeufs à la coque* or soft-boiled eggs in a shell every morning at first light. Along with a whole loaf of freshly baked French bread. Soon Rusty, too, had adopted the habit and used the bread to dip into the runny egg yolk, making the contents overflow.

All six Frenchmen smoked fancy European meerschaum pipes manufactured this side of the Bosporus River in Turkey. They wore well-used buckskin clothing and walking boots. They seemed more heavily armed than normal for an expedition, but maybe they knew more about what lay ahead than the two Americans. As they prepared to get underway, smoked swirled around their heads, and everybody was grinning like a possum. Capt. Rusty Steel checked the steam in the boilers and threw the levers setting the left paddle into gear. It gently pushed them off the dock and into the flowing river. He turned the ship due north as the sun rose into the sky like it was suspended on a string. Bright rays of light slanted through the trees along the river's banks.

Bells sounded from the pilot's house, and the beating of feet were heard as sailors scrambled across the decks to secure the mooring lines, pull the gangplank aboard, and fasten down. The first mate's whistle squealed through the foggy morning. Everything that wasn't tied down tended to move about with the shifting of the waters. If they ran into a sand bar, all the cargo would be tossed around, but Rusty Steel knew these waters like the back of his hand. Later in the voyage, he would find making way more challenging, but on those first days, it was like a pleasure ride. He didn't have all the nagging passengers he usually carried along with cattle and cargo. It would be a pleasure cruise to Kansas City.

The paddleboat required a restock of firewood and water every few days. The initial part of the route had trading posts and friendly Indians along the way. It was relatively well traveled between St. Louis and Kansas City, but the farther north and west they went, the wilder the environment became. They would then turn north, following the river into the higher latitudes.

Late one afternoon, they were searching for a place to moor the ship as the sky darkened with cumulonimbus clouds. The occasional bolt of lightning arched from one cloud to another. Finally, large raindrops hit the deck and exploded like tiny bombs. The teak oil made the first drops bead up and roll down the deck. Soon, the drizzle turned into a downpour as streams of water ran along the decks, out the scuppers, and into the river.

When the heavens opened and the rains came in earnest, things got complicated as the river rose, increasing its flow, and all sorts of broken logs and branches swiftly floated downstream in the direction of the *Dragon Queen's* bow. Now the riverbank where they would usually moor up and weather the storm was underwater, and they had to continue at an idle as a dozen men with lanterns looked into the murky waters for signs of danger.

Nobody got any sleep that night, but with the sun came the end of the rain. The only signs of rainfall were the roaring river and the rainbow in the distance. The dark low-hanging clouds opened to clear blue skies, and during the course of the day, the river went down again. They continued to chug onward against the stiff current of three to five miles per hour, slowing their headway and burning more wood.

Captain Steel knew everything would change when they passed the Yankton Sioux camp. Rusty knew Louis and Clark had previously visited it, and they had met no resistance. The Indians lived on a Missouri River Bluff. There they would have to stop and take on wood and water. At this point, steamboat traffic was rare so far north, where the waters were relatively unchartered and deceiving.

Even Rusty finally ran the *Dragon Queen* aground. When he had taken over the original *Dragon Queen* upon the death of Captain Bligh, he traded her in for a newer model and rechristened her with the same name. Now he found himself with his aging vessel hung up on a large sandbar invisible under the water's surface.

Many paddleboats were lost on the Mississippi and Missouri Rivers. Some ships lasted no more than four or five years, while others with an expert captain lasted ten years and more. The tricky business of navigating these waters kept the risk of losing a vessel constantly in the back of a skipper's mind. When they ran aground, the breakable cargo was saved because the first mate had made sure everything was tethered down.

Captain Steel threw both paddles into reverse and pushed the throttles to full speed, but the ship still didn't move. He ran one forward and the other in reverse until he feared the boiler would blow. There was only one way left to lift the paddle boat off the sandbar. He was going to have to grasshopper the ship.

"We're gonna have to walk the boat over the sandbar. I doubt it'll rain again as it's getting too late in the season, and the nights are already cold, so we might wait here for two weeks before the river rises enough to float us off this sandbar."

The first mate nodded as his brow furrowed. They all knew if they lost the paddleboat now, the journey would be over before it had even gotten interesting. They would have to return overland, and anything could happen. Everybody was as serious as a heart attack.

"Do you think ya can pull it off, Captain?" First Mate Gordon asked.

"With a little bit of luck, I reckon I can do it," Rusty replied as he eyed the water through the pilothouse window.

Walking the boat was a way of lifting the bow of a steamboat like it was on crutches. It worked best with double-wheel paddleboats.

"We've got to get it up and down the sandbank with poles, blocks, and the strong rigging at the top," Captain Steel said. "We'll use the paddlewheels to lift and move the ship through successive steps from the helm. Leverage those long planks in the paddles like crutches. When you've got it all in place, sound your whistle, and we'll try to walk her across. Easy now as we gotta make it across step by step until we're afloat again. If we poke a hole in the boat's hull, the party is over. Push those planks forward from the bow on either side of the boat and into the sandbar at as much angle as possible. Near the end of each pole, secure a block with a strong rope that can pass through the pulleys that lower another pair of blocks attached to the deck near the bow."

The end of each line went to a winch, which when turned, wound tight, and with its weight on the stringers, it slightly raised the boat's bow. Rusty activated the paddlewheels and moved the ship ahead a baby step—but it worked.

They struggled with the paddleboat the entire afternoon, but just like Captain Steel said he could—he got her off the sandbar, and they were chugging up the river again against the current. It was laborious and tricky work for the crew, but now they could continue to the Indian camp.

Finally, they arrived at the Yankton Sioux camp. It was the largest Indian camp Rusty and his first mate had ever seen. A hundred streams of black smoke rose into the sky from fires as far as they could see, and beside them, the ground was dotted with teepees. Dozens of men, women, and children gathered on the riverbank to see who the white people were and what they had to trade. The number of Native Americans made the crew of the *Dragon Queen* nervous, but the French seemed to know some of the people and even a little of their language. Apparently, Jean-Luc was more experienced than he let on to be.

Monsieur Vonore dropped off the side of the paddleboat and into waist-deep water as he trudged his way up the riverbank and the awaiting Indians. His five French friends joined him. They had strings of beads wrapped around their necks and arms and were offering them to the Sioux. They appeared to know them better than Rusty expected. The first twinge of suspicion buried inside him like a worm. A bad feeling began to eat at his stomach as he watched the Sioux flash glances at the ship and all the cargo.

Even though he sensed something wasn't right, he couldn't put a finger on it. Now, Rusty wondered what was inside the crates the Frenchmen had stored aboard. He began to feel he had been used and tricked into doing something he shouldn't have, but how was he to know? He shot a glance over his shoulder at his first mate, Mr. Gordon. When their eyes met, he knew he felt the same.

Rusty had heard rumors of Frenchmen smuggling guns to the Indians to use against the other white men in the area. The French sought to trick the Sioux into doing what they wanted and hired them as an additional army in some cases of rebellion. The Indians would pay a pretty penny for a few hundred muskets. Unfortunately, Rusty believed he had been duped and was involved in transporting illegal weapons to the Sioux—guns that would eventually be used on men like him. Men who only sought to be free and live a peaceful life. Now Rusty's own life had been turned around.

Rusty slowly backed up toward Chuck without taking his eyes off the Frenchmen. At this point, he believed he needed to confirm what he thought to be true.

"Here, Chuck, put my hat and coat on and keep your face in the shade of the brim," Rusty whispered. "We don't want the Frenches to discover you're not me while I head belowdecks and check out what's in those crates."

In less than ten seconds, they had exchanged hats and coats, and

Captain Steel raced down the gangway to the ladder, to the bottom decks, and finally to the cargo hold and stables. He had already walked through the cargo area the day they departed, but that was to ensure it was all secure and that nothing was tipped over. Then he noticed the crates but hadn't thought twice about it.

The Frenchmen seemed so genuine in their intentions and as friendly as any men they had met. When they got to the first stack of long crates, his wild eyes shot around him to ensure he was alone. He drew a long, heavy-bladed knife and pried the top off the first box he found. The nails screeched as the wood pulled free. He whipped his head around to see if anybody had heard.

When he looked inside, at first glimpse, he only saw straw, but as he explored further, pushing the filling away, he uncovered a box of six flintlock long rifles. There were sixteen such boxes stacked in the hold. He imagined some of the barrels weren't full of flour but would hold gun powder. There would be lead balls, too. Jean-Luc Vonore planned to arm the Indians to fight against the Americans as they pushed their way westward with the Louisiana Purchase. He was attempting to form a resistance.

He turned on his heels and ran for the deck where he had left Chuck, but when he got close, he saw the Sioux had already detained him. Twenty men had snuck up on the paddleboat, scaled its low gunnels, and captured his sailors, including Mr. Gordan. The Indians must have thought he was the captain. They led them through the water to the riverbank and apparently hostile Indians. The Frenchmen now held guns in their hands.

Rusty pushed his brace of pistols deep into his belt, grabbed the first rifle he saw, and slipped it over his shoulder. Then he turned for the boiler room at a dead run. Steel knew he only had seconds before they discovered he was missing. He opened the valves to the boilers to increase the steam. He slung a kerosene lamp into the corner and tossed a match to set it afire. He ran back to the deck and plugged his powder horn tight. Then he moved from one shadow to the other and silently slipped into the murky waters of the Missouri River.

Lucky for him, he had learned to swim all those years ago after nearly drowning. Captain Bligh was an intricate and complex man, but he had spared his life just the same. He had even given him a second chance as well. Steel would have grown into a scoundrel if it hadn't been for him and may even be dead by now. Now he mentally thanked him for forcing him to learn to swim.

The riverboat captain silently slipped below the water and swam under the surface as far as he could. His powerful strokes quickly brought him close to the far bank. His lungs began to burn, but he forced his lips to close tighter and continued with his long, even strokes. He realized he was on the other shore when his head bumped into the bank. Amidst the stand of canes, he pushed his head barely out of the water. Now he could see the Indians forcing his crew out of the water and toward the Frenchmen—the waiting enemies of the state. There was little Rusty Steel could do about it, though.

He watched as Chuck made a break for it but was struck down by a Frenchman. He shot him in his tracks.

Rusty cut a cane stalk, then he submerged again, using it as a straw to breathe through. He held onto the plants so the four-knot current didn't take him downstream. He knew the Frenchmen wouldn't return to Kansas City or St. Louis. He knew it wouldn't be long before the French traitors found Chuck wasn't him and that he had escaped. He believed, first, they would search the boat. He remembered the old saying, a captain always goes down with his ship. Well, not if he can avoid it. It was pure luck he had gotten away. If he hadn't checked the guns and traded jackets with Gordon, he would be in the hands of the enemy Frenchmen and Sioux right now.

He knew there was nothing he could do about his first mate. There were hundreds of Indians, plus the six heavily armed French fighters. These men weren't interested in trapping. The crates that were supposed to carry the traps held long rifles to arm their enemies, whoever they might be.

Rusty doubted the Indians would chase him, but he figured the Frenchmen would. Steel knew too much about these men and even had the leader's name. They would want to make sure he was dead, as dead men don't talk. He knew he had to run fast and far but not before he got revenge for his first mate, Gordon. Now that he had his sights set on heading to the mountains, he ran for Montana. He would make sure the Frenchmen were chasing him, and he would pick them off one at a time. Rusty knew he could never return to St. Louis as he would be disgraced for allowing himself to be tricked into such a situation. His boredom had allowed him to be talked into a fake fantasy.

He had been duped into believing they were going on a fur-trapping expedition. Now that he looked back, he remembered Jean-Luc's hands weren't as scarred and scratched as those of other trappers he had seen. He should have smelled a rat right off, but he was lured in by the rewards of both money and adventure.

Rusty stopped for a moment to catch his breath and get his bearings. It would be night soon, and he needed to get out of the water before hypothermia struck him down. He built a fire deep in a gorge and dried his clothes as best he could. Then he would find a hollowed-out tree where he would sleep for a few hours until the sliver of moon rose again, and he would continue. He doubted the Frenchmen would venture out into the dark to search for him—it would be too dangerous. They would come for him as fast as they could at first light. Pain shot up his shoulders and legs from the cold river water.

Rusty climbed the far bank in the dark, hid behind a tree, and waited. He knew something should happen soon, or his final blow to the French rebels would have failed. The blast was heard for miles as a fireball erupted from the steam engine's boiler and rose into the sky, turning the fading day into light, if only for a moment. Flames shot into the sky, and suddenly the entire boat was catching fire so quickly it looked surreal. Of course, the old wooden paddleboat was as flammable as a tinder box. The boilers had blown out the guts, and the kerosene had assured the fire. The blast spread burning debris throughout the lower decks of the steamship.

Rusty Steel watched as everyone on the bank dove for the ground, burying their faces in the dirt. Debris was thrown across the camp, spreading fire to the teepees, and chunks of wood slammed into unsuspecting Sioux Indians. Right before their very eyes, the Frenchmen watched as their cargo burst into flames and sank right there in shallow water. The heat from the boilers was so intense, the metal gun barrels were damaged beyond repair. The stocks were no more than ashes, along with their wooden boxes.

Some of the chickens were blown off the deck and miraculously weren't harmed. A dozen chickens and a single rooster strutted up and down the riverbank, poking their beaks into holes, looking for worms. Occasionally the rooster would crow despite the hour. The fireball had turned time upside-down for everybody. Every other living creature was in a panic.

Now was the time for Rusty to run. He knew the Frenchmen were less likely to pursue if he returned to Kansas City. But if he headed deeper into the wilderness, they would surely follow. It was apparent this wasn't the first time they had been there.

3

TURNING THE TABLES

Rusty Steel took advantage of the distraction of the ship's boilers exploding and ran through the dense forest at the river's edge. This made it impossible for anyone to get a bead on him. Between the thick foliage and the dense black smoke, he was invisible. He raced until he felt like his lungs were on fire and his heart was about to explode as it hammered loudly between his ears. It wasn't fear that he now felt. It was pure anger and a clear sense of urgency. Rusty had ruled his ship with an iron fist for decades, and he wasn't about to let some renegade immigrants get away with what they had done.

Little did they know—they had crossed a man they shouldn't have. All they knew of him was that he was a paddleboat captain. None of them imagined his dark past on the wharves of Missouri. If they wanted to play dirty, he knew how to do that, too. He had learned when he was a small boy in the streets of St. Louis where murder was rife—an everyday occurrence. He intended to pay them back for what they had done to his first mate, Chuck Gordon. He doubted he could survive such an injury, and even if he did, he probably wouldn't be able to travel. Burning the *Dragon Queen* was a deed that deserved death, not to mention the lives of his crew. Now only he was left to wreak the wrath on the traitors.

I swear on my life I will see every one of the Frenchmen die—I'll kill them with my bare hands, Rusty Steal thought to himself.

His fists were clenched so tightly his knuckles were white and his mouth no more than a gash. He rested for a moment to catch his breath and listen. He heard nothing over the cicadas as they continued their constant chatter.

As he ran, he left just enough track so the French pirates wouldn't lose the trail but not enough to make them suspicious. Rusty swore at his boots because they hurt his feet. His pants were torn to shreds by thorny bushes. Half-moons of sweat appeared under the arms of his half-dried clothing. The thought crossed his mind that he would have to dress more for his environment. Especially now as the river had reached the bend that led them north and into even more unknown territory. Rusty wondered how far he would have to run along the river before he had the opportunity to snatch the lives away from the tricky Frenchmen. He knew he would have to be careful or find himself the one captured.

That was something that he planned to avoid at all costs. If he failed, he would betray his friends who had lost their lives and his madam, the *Dragon Queen.* So, he would have to be extremely careful and resist the impulse to trudge forward recklessly. He no longer had a ship nor a friend, so he wasn't in any hurry—he had all the time in the world, and he knew the Frenchmen would have to chase him down, or their secret would be divulged. Something that would leave them hanging from the end of a rope.

Rusty had no family waiting for his return. He had lost contact with them long ago. He had one goal in life: the death of the six men who betrayed him and his sailors. They weren't only smugglers and thieves; they were cold-blooded murderers as well. Nothing short of death would suffice for them, and Rusty planned to watch the life leave all their eyes from less than a foot away. They had made this personal, and their actions presented a danger to American settlers. Arming the Indians could only lead to problems. He might not be able to stop it all, but he sure as heck would stop these six. They wouldn't be returning to their homes in Canada or Europe.

Some wouldn't expect a riverboat captain to be very fit. They didn't realize he spent seven days a week climbing ladders from one deck to another and wrestling the massive wheel in the pilothouse. Then there were problems like the sandbars, and you always had someone on the boat who would choose to get out of order. This usually happened in the saloon on the top deck and was the responsibility of the captain along with the first mate. Captain Steel was a dead shot with both pistols and his long rifle. This was something he had to prove time and again over the years.

Rusty was a changed man from the boy of his past. But he tapped into his violent and cruel feelings from boyhood when required. He used the resulting anger to make his body do what his mind wanted.

When he knew he had enough of a lead on the Frenchmen, he circled around and got behind them. He noticed their track indicated they were moving fast. They probably thought they were about to catch up. He carefully tailed the last man strung out in the line on the narrow path. He had chosen this route so they would have to travel in a single file. That left the man on drag an easy target.

When Rusty clamped his hand over his mouth and pushed the blade between his ribs, he gasped for air. It felt like there was a searing fire inside his lungs. The captain stared deep into the Frenchman's eyes. He looked back in recognition. He realized they had mistaken him for somebody who would be easy to kill. This Marseillais knew he had made a mistake following this man, but now it was too late. He exhaled as the blade sliced through his heart. The captain still held his hand over his mouth when he heard his throat rattle; he watched the light go out in his eyes like he had promised. Now there was one down and only five more to go.

Rusty left the body on the trail so it would be easy for the French traitors to find it. He wanted to anger them, making them reckless while he kept his cool and planned how to take the next man. Now they would watch their backs, but he knew their eyes couldn't be everywhere. As he ran past a stand of dried-out cane, he stopped and chopped down several and cut them into pieces about two feet long. Now he swung wide of the Frenchmen and ran as hard as he could through the forest. Branches and thorns cut his face and hands and tore his clothing even more.

JEAN-LUC VONORE WAS the first one to suspect something was amiss. They had stopped to rest and eat some food. They even made a kettle of coffee to give them the energy to rush on until they caught the man who knew who they were. It was imperative for them to kill him before he could tell the army what they did and where to find them. If not, it would only be a matter of time before they were discovered.

When their drag man didn't arrive after half an hour, Jean-Luc said, "Stay here and keep sharp. I'm going to look and see what happened to Pierre."

Jean-Luc pulled his pistols and backtracked down the trail. Now he was a little more careful, but he believed he would find his fellow countryman tending to his personals or something as innocent. Blood pooled beneath the dead body when he saw it. He hadn't been dead long. He was still warm. Pierre had been stabbed in the back by an unseen assailant.

Of course, Indians also populated these forests, and some lay in wait for trespassers. He couldn't rule that out, although he had a sneaking suspicion that Mister Rusty might have had something to do with it. Maybe there was more to the man than met the eye.

Jean-Luc debated if he should bury his Christian brother. They had grown up together in the Catholic church in southern France. He knew they didn't have the time. If he stopped to dig a hole and say some words over his grave, the captain would get away. He looked for tracks beside the trail and saw where Captain Steel had cut around and headed north again. Now was the time to catch him. They must be able to run faster than an old man who spent his days at the wheel of his ship. Or maybe it was some Indian warriors. There were plenty of tribes around, and they knew they weren't all sympathetic to the French. The Pawnee and the Cheyenne were two such tribes.

When he returned to the remaining four comrades, he hissed,

"We lost Pierre. Now we have to make up for the lost time. We can't let an old man outrun us, can we? We are French, and he is only an uncouth American. Lance, you take the point, and I will take drag. I dare anyone to try to catch me unawares."

Lance jumped to his feet and took off down the trail so he could get a lead on his fellow compatriots. He carried his pistols in his hands and was ready to use them. If it was the white man, then so bit it. He would murder him on sight. If it was Indians, he would try to bargain first; then, he would use his guns, knowing his four friends were trailing close behind him.

Lance maintained a neck-breaking pace. His eyes raced all around, looking for danger anywhere ahead of him. He looked down the trail, on the hills, and even in the trees. If they were Indian, they could be anywhere.

When he stepped on the spikes, he gasped and couldn't catch his breath. When he looked down, he saw two spiked canes sticking through the top of his boots. They had traversed his feet. He finally inhaled deeply to let out a scream—when a large hand clamped tight over his mouth, muffling his voice. The veins popped out all along his neck as the pain dominated his world. It was all he could think about. He blinked his eyes repeatedly, and they finally fell on Rusty's. He felt the blade slip under his ribcage and into his heart. It beat three times, skipped a few beats, spasmed, and stopped. Not a sound was heard from the Frenchman.

In minutes Jean-Luc and his entourage arrived at the slayed body. Now he wasn't sure it was one man and not several Indians. The spike trap looked like something an Indian would do. Now all the men pulled their weapons and looked all around them. For the moment, they forgot the river captain. Then Jean-Luc saw the knife wound in his back. It was the same as Pierre's. Could it really be Rusty Steel who killed his men? All of them and he had been soldiers and sailors both. But now he was beginning to get a bad feeling. It seemed to creep across his soul like a dark and dangerous shadow.

He searched Lance and discovered his weapons were gone. His

pistols and his throwing knife. It had been the same with Pierre. Whoever it was, they were getting better armed with each defeat.

"We aren't going to leave Lance here, too, are we, Jean-Luc? He's my wife's cousin."

"If you value your life, you won't worry about it," Jean-Luc replied. "We can tend to the dead once we've killed whoever is responsible. My bet is it's that American ship captain."

"He didn't look like the type," Françoise said. "I can't believe that unassuming captain killed both Lance and Pierre."

"If we leave them, the wild animals will get to their bodies before we get back to bury them. I would hate to have you leave my body behind like that," Louis said. "I insist we bury the dead. At least Lance. He was like family."

Against the leader's better judgment, Jean-Luc allowed the remaining three men to bury Lance but didn't take his eyes off the trail heading north and south. *Which way should I go?* He asked himself. He already knew the answer, though. He would continue to head north. For some reason, he knew the men he chased would not turn back south. Maybe it was some sort of intuition, but he was sure they were going the right way.

After they finished with some last words, they each made the cross and kissed their thumb and forefinger. Then they all turned and began to jog north along the same trail they were on. Each one now wondered if they were running toward a roaring train. Or was a deadly warrior brave following them? All of them but Jean-Luc believed it was anybody but the captain. Something deep down inside Vonore told him it was the skipper, and there was something beneath that stern facade that they hadn't noticed when they picked him to smuggle their long guns to the Indians. It was like he was suddenly another person, and he wasn't sure they could defeat him.

The only thing Jean-Luc heard was the thud. It didn't even hurt— at least not at first. The blade had slipped through his neck as slick as spit. The hilt of the blade slammed against his neck, alarming him. He raked his fingers at his throat as if he could unblock it and breathe. He felt the tip of hard steel protruding from the other side.

When he touched it, the tip pricked his finger. His eyes became cloudy just before everything went black. But there, in the near distance, he saw a pair of eyes blink. The whites gave away his position in the bushes. He was so close Jean-Luc wondered how he had not seen him. He very nearly stepped on him. Now he was dead.

When the last three Frenchmen saw their leader die such an ugly death right before their eyes, they all turned and ran south back down the trail for what they hoped would be freedom. Now they crowded each other as they all three tried to span the narrow path. They didn't see the trip wire strung across the trail. Suddenly they were all sprawled out on their faces. When they heard the hammers click behind them, hackles sprouted on their necks, and goosebumps popped up on their arms.

"Turn over, scum," Rusty Steel growled. He pointed the barrels of a brace of pistols at the three men on the ground. He had three more pistols in his belt. One had the hammer cocked. Pepe went for his gun. It was his only chance. Two shots rang out simultaneously as bullet holes sprouted from two of the three men's chests. As slick as spit, Rusty dropped one pistol, drew another, and shot the last man between the eyes. He watched the life leave each and every one.

4

MOUNTAIN MEN

After the killings, Rusty kept following the Missouri River right up to the Rocky Mountains. He wasn't quite sure if there would be any repercussions for killing the six Frenchmen. He hardly thought so, but you never knew when it came to courts and the law. He knew he had to do what he did, but with every witness dead and the ship burned, there was no way to prove his actions were proper. Of course, the Indians knew what happened, but who would believe them even if they did allow them into a courtroom? So, he decided to keep on going. Now he was headed for the wilderness. He had had enough of his fellow man and just wanted to explore the tall mountains and live off the land.

Capt. Randy Steel had been responsible for the ship's crew ever since Bligh died, and he was made the captain in his place. The old seadog even arranged for a loan to be available so Steel could purchase the ship, and he wouldn't have to work for someone else. This also guaranteed the crew kept their jobs of many years. Men's families depended on those paychecks, and even though Captain Bligh was ornery, he was a good man deep down inside.

Strangely enough, the riverboat captain excelled in becoming a mountain man, and the lifestyle fit him right down to his boots.

Maybe his destiny hadn't been the river like he had thought all his life. He spent the next decade avoiding civilization and learning what he could from Crow and Ute Indians. The Blackfeet didn't seem to want to have anything to do with him. He climbed the highest mountains and traveled to Montana, Colorado, Utah, Wyoming, and South Dakota. He walked as far north as British Colombia and as far south as New Mexico. After a decade, he had come to know every crack and cranny across the Rocky Mountains. He always seemed to be on the go and made no particular place his home.

When he first heard about the Rendezvous, he didn't understand what it was. He had been told of the event by some Crow Indians. They were curing one hundred cold-winter beaver pelts and planned to go.

"Ain't it a mite dangerous for you boys to meet up in a place with so many white men?" Rusty asked his Crow buddy.

"No, my friend," Hachta said. "For many winters, mountain men, Indians, and fur traders have met somewhere in the Rocky Mountains. It is a time of guaranteed peace because all the tribes send braves to purchase steel tools and knives—maybe even a flintlock musket and some powder. Even for an Indian, something that cost twelve of the finest pelts is a dear purchase."

"How many grizzly bear skins are ya holdin' for me now, Hachta?"

"Over the last few years, you have filled my teepee with your bear hides. I have them knee-deep on the floor of my home to keep me warm in the winter. It is time to sell your furs, Rusty Steel. How long has it been since you have spoken to white people—others like yourself?"

The question caught him by surprise, and he had to ponder on it for a moment before he replied, "It must be goin' on ten years, if not more than a decade. The last white men I saw weren't Americans, and the encounter wasn't friendly."

"Yes, upon occasion, you have mentioned such times, but your secret is safe with me. This is not the same, but there might be some French trappers there too. They come down from British Colombia past the northern border where the Rockies meet their country. But at the Rendezvous, nobody is allowed to fight unless it is for competition and fun. Then all things are possible. You can trade some of your furs for a good Hawken rifle. It will serve you better than your old Tennessee long rifle. Then maybe you will trade your gun to me for eight winter beaver pelts."

"That's four less than what it's worth," Rusty replied. "You know as well as I do, it'll fetch twelve or thirteen high-quality beaver skins."

"It's a small price to pay for me keeping your furs all these years," Hachta said, chuckling. "I have taught you the ways of the Crow Indians—even our language. Don't you believe you owe me something for that?"

Rusty laughed and said, "I reckon we can work somethin' out. But only if ya take me with ya to the Rendezvous. I don't fancy goin' it alone. Then we can use your mules, too, because all of them grizzly furs won't fit on mine."

They were snaking down a switchback trail to the Plains below two weeks later. This year the Rendezvous was held at the confluence of Horse Creek and the Green River in Wyoming.

"They've had a few other Rendezvous here, too, but it's not always in Wyoming," Hachta said. "A few years back, they held one in Pierre's Hole, Idaho. The fur trading companies back the event and supply it with whiskey; a means to trade your furs without going down the Mississippi to St. Louis or over to Old Fort Boise. Either that or up to Fort Vancouver in what they call the Pacific Northwest for the British companies. This way, the mountain men and the Indians can stay near their mountains and not have to bother with civilization."

"It's been so long since I spoke English, other than the little bit I've taught you; I figure I might be a little rusty."

"Lucky for me, you learned Crow quickly. I am afraid I am not very good at learning other tribes' tongues."

As soon as they rode into the encampment, they were overwhelmed by its size. Of course, Rusty hadn't seen much more than Indian camps for the last decade, so everything seemed too populated and confusing to him. Heavy oxen-driven wagons pulled barrels of whiskey to the different events. There were knife-throwing and pistol shooting contests, along with long gun sharp-shooting, arm wrestling, darts, and checkers. If somebody knew how and had a mind, they could even play a game of chess. Wagers were placed on all the events. The small bets for hides and skins made the event much more exciting, and the adrenaline levels grew in the crowd.

Mountain men and Indians alike competed in wrestling matches. There was no violence because even this was done in a festive mood. Everything exchanged hands, from beaver pelts to fancy pistols and hand-carved good luck charms—anything a mountain man might find of value. A large tent was assembled where the trading post was found. All sorts of dry goods were for sale or barter, including cherished coffee and store-bought chewing and smoking tobacco.

It also housed a makeshift saloon. Long wooden planks lay across large barrels to make a bar that extended from one end of the tent to the other. Round tables with wooden stools dotted the rest of the covered area. Over a hundred mountain men occupied the seats and the bar as they sipped on high-grade whiskey free of charge.

Hachta and Rusty stopped to watch five men take turns shooting at paper targets. They had to fire ten bullets each in the shortest time possible, hitting the bullseye with every shot. Both men carefully watched when they brought the targets back. Many of the bullet holes were inside the black circle in the middle, but half were an inch or two from dead center.

"I reckon I can do better than that," Rusty whispered to his Crow friend. "I sure have practiced enough. I can reload a gun in twenty seconds flat."

He unstrapped his long rifle from his shoulder and walked up to the group of men. He had to look for the words for a second, but soon enough, they spilled out just like ten years ago.

"What's a man gotta do to place a bet in this contest?" Rusty asked.

"I'm Polecat Jack, and I'm in charge here, mister. Whatcha got ya wanna wager? This here is a new round, boys. We got us a newcomer in our midst. I seen ya lookin' at the targets. You figure you stand a chance, don't cha now?"

"I reckon I might. I'll wager a seven-foot grizzly skin. My Name is Rusty Steel, and my Crow Indian friend here is Hachta, but he don't speak English."

"You don't have to speak English here," Jack replied and grinned. "All you gotta do is shoot straight."

Rusty and five other men put in valuables equal to the grizzly bear skin. It would make someone a good winter coat. They all looked at the newcomer with curiosity.

"Who wants to start?" Jack asked.

"I'm ready," Mountain Dennis Breed said. He walked up to the bails of straw to steady his barrel and took a bead. The rifle recoiled, making a bang, and sent a led bullet through the target, embedding into the hillside behind. It was an inch off-center.

Dennis was a fast loader, but with each reload, his aim suffered. He was rushing the shots by the tenth bullet. When they pulled the target in, eight bullets had hit the black dot in the middle, but none dead center.

Next came Yosemite Bob, who was short and aging with gray hair and a handlebar mustache. He had a fancy hand-engraved rifle with inlayed stock. He was slightly better than Dennis, but neither man hit the center once.

Syracuse Sam wore a thick raccoon skin cap with the tail intact. Scar tissue was visible an inch above his eyebrows. He seemed to move slowly, but his reload was so smooth he beat the other two by ten seconds, and all his bullets were inside the black bullseye, and two were dead center.

Next came Angus McFarlin. His tall and gangly frame swaggered over to take his place. He carried his rifle over his shoulder with the barrel in his hand.

"Now let me show y'all how it's done," Angus said with a heavy southern drawl.

He licked his thumb, wet the gunsight, and then put the stock to his shoulder. He made all ten shots in three minutes and forty seconds. Angus fired and reloaded quicker than his fellow mountain men, but his aim was reckless. When they examined his target, his friends immediately began to hack on him and make fun, but he seemed to be too happy to get angry—he was grinning like a Cheshire cat.

"It looks like you got your work cut out for ya, stranger," Polecat Jack smiled as he eyed Rusty. "I wonder who's gonna take that nice grizzly skin home to make 'em a warm winter coat?" He grinned some more and waved his hand to make way for Rusty.

The mountain man from St. Louis shot, reloaded, and fired—he worked like a well-oiled machine. His competitors were left with their jaws hanging to their chins. When Jack brought the paper target back, he was shaking his head.

"I never seen the likes," Jack said. "Eight out of ten are dead center, with the other two an inch off. Three minutes and thirty-eight seconds in all. That's a record in my book."

All the hardy mountain men patted Rusty on the back and congratulated him. He picked through his winnings, and he found a watch. It made him chuckle. It obviously hadn't worked in some years.

"Here, Hachta," Rusty said, "this one's for you. I ain't got no use for a watch even if it did work."

Everybody laughed. Especially Dennis, who had used it to cover his bet. "It'll make a dandy necklace, won't it?"

After all the men participating finished, Rusty had beaten all five hands down. That was also the day he made a dozen new friends, and all of them were mountain men who lived much like himself.

"And what do you win, Jack?" Rusty asked.

"Why, I get paid by the American Fur Company. They pay for all this just so we'll sell them our furs to take back to St. Louis or up north. That's who paid for the whiskey this year, too. They set up the trading post and all, so we don't have to venture back east. Here we trade and barter, but mostly we have fun. But they ain't fools. They get the beaver pelts at the best price in the market as they buy from the source."

"How long you been doin' this, Jack?" Rusty asked.

"I reckon it's been nigh on a decade by now," Polecat replied.

"Why don't you and your friend come along with us? Maybe we can find another shootin' match and catch us an unsuspecting target," Dennis said and winked. "Don't worry, Rusty. This week is the only time in the year that everybody is only out to sell their furs and have fun. Soon folks will be dancing and carryin' on somethin' fierce. A little fun mixed in with a little business is always good for the soul."

"I see some of my Crow cousins over there," Hachta said to Rusty in Crow. "I'll catch up."

"You speak Crow Indian, do ya?" Dennis asked as he took a second look at the mountain man in front of him.

Rusty nodded his head.

His long beard fluttered in the breeze. Even before they knew the man, they knew there was something about him that immediately garnered respect. It looked like he had spent the last years with the Indians. He dressed like a Crow.

Rusty Steel and his newfound friends competed, drank, ate, and traded until the event's last day. When it was time to go, Rusty was torn between heading back with Hachta or heading off somewhere else. Maybe somewhere he hadn't explored. Now he would have to refresh his supply of furs and pelts too. He would have to hunt for bears before they hibernated and the beaver in the mountain streams in the dead of winter.

"Why don't cha tag along with us for a spell, Rusty?" Dennis asked. "I can guarantee you'll have more fun than huntin' and trap-pin' on your own."

Mountain Dennis had taken a liking to Rusty straight off, and all of them were impressed with his shooting skills and the furs he brought down to trade. They were all perfectly cured, and the bear skins were massive.

"What do you say?" Rusty asked Hachta in Crow. "Do you mind heading back up the mountain alone?"

"I have my cousins to return home with. They need my mules

because they have bought half the trading post. I saw a Hawken rifle for sale in the trading post."

"You owe me eight winter beaver pelts," Rusty said as he gave his rifle to his friend. "You can give 'em to me next summer. If I don't see ya before, then we can meet here."

Hachta nodded, smiled, turned, and headed to collect his string of mules.

"I didn't understand a thing you said, so is that a yes or a no?" Dennis asked as he chuckled.

"I reckon I could use some company for hunting and trapping this winter," Rusty said. "It's been a long time since I rode with anybody. I only see a few Crow Indian friends now and then, and if I head over to the west, I've got a couple of Ute friends. Sometimes I've gone a year without speakin' to a single soul."

YEARS LATER, Rusty and his five mountain man friends were waiting in the Wichita Trading Post. They didn't usually have much to do with the military, but they had heard about a ruckus some army boys started with the Comanche war party. That and something about them burning a wagon train of settlers. After that, there was nowhere safe to travel unless you were well armed and in numbers. Everybody was afraid of the Comanche—even the mountain men. They hooked up with the soldiers on what they claimed was an expedition. By the time they arrived at this year's Rendezvous, they had lost nearly half their men, and among them were some of the most important.

The annual event attracted as many as five hundred people. All of them were trappers and traders who worked in the Rocky Mountains. A number of Native Americans were present too. There were folks there with good intentions. Then there was the Canadian-based Hudson's Bay Company, which tried to destroy the American Fur Company owned by John Jacob Astor. Both were rivals. With the presence of competing firms, the trappers got better prices when the bidding started. Each company tried to outbuy the other. The problem was the Canadian company could offer manufactured trade goods at much better prices than the American fur companies, so many mountain men went where they got the best exchange.

Donald Mackenzie, a Scottish-Canadian fur trader and trailblazer, held the first Rendezvous in the Boise River Valley in 1819. After that, William Henry Ashley of the Rocky Mountain Fur Company organized a regular Rendezvous circuit. Another competitor to accompany the larger businesses.

A famous mountain man by the name of Jim Beckwourth described the Rendezvous in the St. Louis newspapers as *mirth, songs, dancing, trading, target shooting, yarns, frolic with all sorts of extravagances that men or Indians could invent.*

Eventually, ministers began to attend and became regular features, including the Reverend Samuel Parker. They set up tents and spread the Word of the Good Book with their yearly revivals.

5

THE PARTY

The fires were lit as soon as the sun blushed red on the western hillsides, and the Rendezvous was thrown into full swing. It was a warm summer's day with a dimming blue sky above. In minutes a carpet of stars rolled across the heavens chasing away the light. When the full moon rose in the west, it was so large it looked like it was painted on the sky. Its silver glow cast shadows across the valley. Cicadas chattered their choir as crows cawed at the intrusion. Barrels of whiskey stood by an open bar as massive buckskin-clad men drank, danced, and competed.

Whether it was wrestling or shooting, everything seemed to be a competition. The fur trading companies footed the bill because they made the most profits since they had the first bid and selection of the very best cold-weather beaver pelts money could buy. Only the highest-quality cured hide brought top dollar. With a dozen, you could buy a Johnson model 1836 flintlock pistol.

Cookfires dotted the large Rendezvous area as elk stakes sizzled on spits and stew brewed in large cast-iron pots. Long strings of bacon hung over steel rods as orange coals glowed below them while two women made frying-pan biscuits all day and night. The company sponsoring the food stands and bars had their firm's names painted on brightly colored canvases. The Canadians were the most generous as they had the most to earn with their quality products at unbeatable prices.

Levi Beaver Johnson and Bill Forrester walked around the crowd of strangely dressed men and women as they marveled at what they saw. Not only were there dozens of different competitions taking place, but there were also mountains of supplies waiting to be traded for furs. Men dressed much like Levi were everywhere they looked. Many led mule trains and were all heavily laden with hides, furs, and pelts.

"Is the army still gonna pay me my wages?" Levi asked as he looked at his friend and chuckled. "You can't expect a guide to work for nothing."

"Don't worry, Beaver," Forrester said. "I remembered you. Before I sent the sergeant off with my resignation, I gave him the army's money belt, but I took yours and my wages first. They can settle their wages out back at Fort Scott. I doubt there will be a pension in my future after all that happened. If we don't take our pay now, I doubt the army would be very generous considering the situation. They will only think about their monetary losses and not about the lives of men they didn't know."

"I sure hope your soldiers don't have trouble like we did getting here. There were a few moments there I thought we wouldn't make it."

"Nearly half of us didn't," Bill Forrester huffed. "That was a complete disaster. The Comanche nearly wiped us out before we could kill them. I doubt that there'll be any more, though. They were a long way from home. It had their desired effect if they were trying to push men off the Plains. They sent us packing with our tails between our legs."

"Don't worry about it, Captain," Levi said. "You did everything you could. At least you got half of us across alive—that's something to be proud of. Those hostiles weren't just any Indians—they were Comanche. It just wasn't meant to be. It's a mite wilder out here than we had thought. I made most of the trip without much of a hitch except for some thieves. The last bit was something else, though."

"What did you think about them five mountain men you outshot at the shootin' contest?" Bill asked. "And don't call me captain anymore. I'm just another civilian now."

"All right, Captain," Levi laughed. He knew he would always be the captain to him. "I didn't beat them at the competition, but I did outshoot 'em with the targets. Look on the bright side of things. We've still got our scalps, pard."

"Let's go see if they don't have some new rifles or pistols. Maybe they'll have a couple of those Colt revolving carbines. They have an external chamber that rotates every time it's cocked. A single rifle has six shots."

"Don't you think there will be something better to spend your money on?" Levi asked.

"You just saw first-hand how dangerous it is to travel this far west," Captain Bill said. "If we have more bullets, all the better. We can keep our old long rifles to shoot grizzly bears and elk, but the repeater rifles will protect us better against hostile Indians or bandits like your encounter. We'll have six shots each, plus our braces of pistols and a long rifle each. A total of eighteen rounds. That's a passel of bullets.

"That's exactly the point," the captain said. "With more bullets, we can travel with fewer men and have the same results. Traveling without twenty people in tow will make us much less noticeable."

"I agree with the logic, but I sure do hope we don't run into as much trouble as we had to get here," Levi said. "Maybe we can side-kick up with those mountain men we met at the shooting competition. I believed we gained their respect with the contest."

"You gained their respect," Bill replied. "To them, I'm always gonna be an army captain." He spat into the dirt like he had a bad taste in his mouth.

"I can think of worse things to be called than captain," Levi laughed. "Let's go have a look at the trading post and see what they've got that we can use. I don't even know where to go from here. Maybe we can get some local information while we are at it."

A pair of towering men stood guard at either side of the trading post entrance. When they entered the British Colombia trading post, they were overwhelmed with all the goods. There were mountains of everything you could imagine, and it was so full of mountain men making their purchases that it made their heads spin. In the corner were twenty men looking over and discussing different types of rifles and pistols. That was where the boys wanted to be.

"Do you think there will be anything left by the time they get to us?" Captain Bill asked.

Beaver Johnson seemed to be nearly overwhelmed. He had dreamt of mountain men and what they would be like almost his entire life, and here he was in a room with dozens of men dressed like him. When they pushed their way into the corner where the armory was, they immediately saw Mountain Dennis Breed holding a Colt Carbine rifle like they had been talking about. Each of his five friends had one in their hands, too.

"There's the champ, boys," Dennis yelled as he waved for Levi to join him. "The only man I've ever seen outshoot Rusty Steel."

Rusty was standing right next to Dennis along with the other four of the gang, and at first, Levi thought he might be put out by the near loss. Especially to such a young man. As soon as Rusty got sight of Beaver, he grinned from ear to ear, though. Instead of envy, the men showed their respect for any man who could compete with the champion of the Rendezvous of many years. They still had their old champ, but it was clear that next year Rusty would have a hard time beating the young sharpshooter, Beaver Johnson.

"Have a look at this 1836 Colt Carbine, Beaver," Dennis said. "It holds six shots, and all ya gotta do is pull back the hammer, and the chamber turns all on its own. Now, ain't that somethin'?"

Levi took the offered weapon and studied it like the professional he was. He inspected the rotating chamber and marveled at the simplicity of it all.

"Soon, they'll be making pistols like this here rifle, too," Levi said.

"She sure is a beauty. The captain and me were just coming to see if they had any on sale."

"Here, you'll find things you won't find elsewhere," Rusty replied. "The fur trading companies want to keep us happy and from wandering off our mountains. They get the pelts at the prices they need to make a profit. We, in turn, get to have one fine party every spring or summer."

"There ain't but a couple left that ain't reserved, young fella," the trading post clerk said. "I can give you each one, but you best hurry. By midnight I reckon they'll all be gone. Colt made less than a thousand of 'em, so they're mighty scarce to find."

Levi's eyes were drawn to the fifty-caliber Hawken rifle on the wall. He had read all about this rifle, but he never had the need for a gun to kill massive animals like buffalo and grizzly bears. This gun would do the trick from five hundred yards if your aim was good enough, which Beaver's was.

Captain Bill examined the carbine while the store clerk handed Levi the buffalo gun with the octagon barrel. It weighed over fifteen pounds. The trapper and hunter's eyes lit up as soon as he had the massive weapon in his hands. Johnson already knew what he wanted.

"How much for the Hawken, mister?" Levi asked.

"You've got a sharp eye, young man," the clerk replied. "What kind of furs have ya got to trade?"

"I'm afraid I ain't got a fur one for sale, but I've got a couple of double eagles."

The clerk was hesitant to take money when he was here to trade his treasured and inaccessible goods for valuables. Luckily Rusty Steel came to his rescue.

"Let's throw the whole lot in together, and you give us one price. We've got plenty of furs. We can settle with these young friends of ours when the tradin' is done," Rusty said.

All six mountain men and the clerk dickered and groaned at offers for nearly an hour, but they finally agreed. Each of the seven got a Colt carbine, and Levi got his revered Hawken mountain man's rifle, the most powerful long gun available in the United States. Few hunters had the need for such a weapon unless they were headed for the Great Plains or the Rocky Mountains.

It was the only weapon you could depend on to tackle a seven-hundred-pound grizzly bear just as easily as a bull bison at fifteen hundred pounds. With his skills and their current arsenal, there was no stopping them. Levi had even shown the six new friends how he fashioned better beaver traps and gave them a whiff of his special bait. The rugged and experienced mountain men seemed just as eager to have some new blood in their group as the pair of newcomers.

They treated Levi with respect only found in equals and tolerated the captain because he was with Beaver. They also knew he was honorable as they had seen his bravery and organizational skills when the Comanche war party attacked them.

Since they left the British Columbia Trading Post together, Levi and Bill followed. They were all armed to the teeth, but each one had a broad smile on his face. Now for some more fun.

"What are you good at, Captain?" Rusty Steel asked. "Can ya shoot the eyes off a dragonfly like Beaver here?"

No matter how much Bill Forrester disliked being called captain after his disgrace, he couldn't part with his army boots, britches, and hat slapped up on one side. That and his saber were presented to him by his peers at West Point. He found it hard to get his arms around the fact that what he expected to be his career was now in shambles. The expedition that was intended to reach the shores of the Pacific Ocean was doomed by the Comanche. A small fortune was spent on organizing such a journey, and the captain had failed miserably at executing his orders.

Now he found himself torn between the man he thought he was and where he was in his life right now. In half of the empty glass was all he had lost in the blink of an eye. All those years studying and then the patrols from the frontier forts to prepare him for what lay ahead. Little did he know there was no way to prepare for what had happened. He had failed his men and instead went back and got demoted, then publicly drummed out of the army; he chose to disappear into the mountains with his new friend.

Now he even questioned his friendship with Levi Johnson. He was a much different man than Forrester. He was a natural in the wild because he had grown up in the wilderness and was an expert shot. Two things that the captain wasn't. Now he pondered on the question Rusty had asked. What was he good at in a situation like here in the Rendezvous?

"I can ride and use my sword," Captain Forrester replied. "If there's such a contest, I reckon I can put up a good show if not win."

"I think the Indians got a pony race while shooting bows and arrows and throwing lances and tomahawks," Portland Pete said. "Maybe they'll let ya play."

"With that big ole white stallion you got, you may just be able to outrun those Indian ponies," Syracuse Sam said, "but can you use that saber of yours while at a run?"

"You're gonna need something the Indians want to trade," Angus McFarlin said. "Indians ain't got nothin' to do with cash money. Shucks, there ain't nowhere to spend it."

"I've got my old rifle," Bill replied. "That should be worth a bunch of pelts."

"I doubt they'll be able to resist such a bet. You could be losing your gun, ya know," Dennis said and chuckled. "Then again, you just bought yourself a new one, didn't ya?"

"You best go get that white horse of yours, Captain," Rusty smiled. "Now we're gonna see what you're made of, young man."

The horse races were held on the far end of the event and downwind, so the dust clouds from horses' hooves hammering the ground didn't disturb the other events.

6

CAPTAIN FORRESTER

When they arrived, several Indians from different tribes raced by on spotted ponies. Dozens of spectators shouted and whistled, encouraging their favorites onward. Side bets were common even among the Indian games. As they flew by the targets like bullets, they shot arrows from under their horses' necks. Their riding skills and marksmanship were something that left the mountain men in awe.

"No wonder they gave us a shellacking back there on the trail," Rusty said as he watched another set of braves charge past. "Those fellas look like they were born and raised on the back of a horse."

"Them Indians be buffalo hunters," Dennis said. "They race those massive beasts down on horseback and shoot 'em dead with arrows. Do you think you be up to this lot, Captain?"

Suddenly Forrester's confidence fell away like the autumn leaves on a tree. Rusty tugged at his long beard as he stared at the young ex-army officer. Now it was his turn to be put to the test. Each man there had remarkable skills. Obviously, killing Comanche wasn't one of the captain's, so he'd better be an expert at something to be admired by the men present. Most of them had never heard of West Point and probably couldn't even read, and none of them were particularly partial to soldiers who told them what to do. At least this one was as humble as prune pie.

When the captain came prancing back with his stallion, all the Indians stopped and looked. There were Crow, Ute, Pawnee, and Sioux Indians, among others. This was a peaceful way to show off their skills to men who may be their enemies out in the wilderness someday. There was much more at stake for these warriors and hunters. For them, the honor of winning an event was more important than the things that were to be wagered. To win their trophies would be in song and gossip. The proof was the object wagered.

Everyone admired the white stallion and almost immediately disliked the white man, who was obviously an army officer. A long-bladed sword hanging from his belt was proof.

"Who's in charge here?" Rusty asked and grinned. He shot a glance back at the captain—he seemed to have turned a shade paler than before.

A man who appeared to be half white and half Indian replied in perfect English, "I am. My name is Tatter. Do you boys know how to use bows and arrows?"

Tatter laughed, obviously unimpressed, and it rippled through the crowd of Indians. Some even pointed at the soldier and sneered. Their dislike for the military was evident. Most of their encounters with army patrols had been bad experiences. Sometimes someone was killed, too, and it was usually an Indian.

"Why did your parents call ya Tater?" Angus asked, too curious to resist. He had the attention span of a bluegill fish. "That's what we call potatoes back home."

"Because I was the smallest of my brothers, so my pa called me Tatter. I took after my ma, and my brothers took after my pa. My ma calls me White Feather." He sucked on his quid and spat a yard of brown juice into the dirt.

"The captain here wants to wager his rifle if'n y'all be interested," Rusty said. "How many beaver pelts are one of those braves willin' to wager?"

"I've never seen a soldier that could shoot an arrow, so what does he want to do as a challenge?" Tatter asked—everybody looked at Captain Forrester.

Bill felt like his body was shrinking. Dozens of eyes were staring at him, waiting on an answer. What was he going to say? He wasn't a racetrack rider, but he was fast, and his horse was even faster. He felt the grip on his saber.

Then he bucked himself up and thought, *it can't get any worse than what I've already experienced.*

"Do you have any watermelons?" the captain asked.

The Indians looked at him puzzled as soon as Tatter translated what he said.

"I reckon I can scare up a few if'n you need 'em," Tatter replied, then whispered something in Crow to the boy next to him, and the kid scrambled off. "Whatcha got in mind, mister?"

"Six watermelons on wooden posts," the captain said. "We race to see who can destroy the melons and win the race. The posts are to be five feet tall, and the watermelon represents an opponent's head."

Another murmur ran through the crowd of spectators of all colors. This was one of the most exciting events of the day so far, but it just got more interesting. The event they were watching suddenly seemed to become more personal, like they were playing war games and not hunting games. Now the captain had everybody's attention.

"Them braves know how to use their tomahawks, son," Rusty said and grinned from ear to ear. "Let's see what they taught you back East in the soldiers' school. Be careful now. Indians believe a little cheating in sport is fair game."

"If I lose, somebody gets my rifle," the captain said loud enough for everybody to hear, and for a moment, it went so silent, each man could hear himself breathe.

Forrester held his long gun up in the air for all the braves to see. Now it was more like a roar that ran through the crowd. Everybody wanted the rifle, but they knew it would be costly. Nobody parted with a gun in the Rocky Mountains lightly. The Indians looked at each other and whispered among themselves. Who would be the highest bidder winning the right to compete for the rifle? That and the honors of embarrassing a white pony soldier.

Five braves jumped forward, offering everything from beaver pelts to marten, fox, bear, and raccoon skins. One poor Indian trapper even offered fifty muskrat furs when any fool knew it took twenty of the low-quality furs to trade for one cold-weather beaver pelt.

"The highest bet of them all was twenty top-quality beaver skins. These be pelts trapped in the dead of winter," Tatter said like he could hardly believe the wager from Black Bear.

Both bets—the pelts and the gun—were an unheard-of wager among the Indians. The two Sioux who made the highest wager walked forward. The leader of the two was tall for an Indian—nearly eye-to-eye with Captain Forrester. He led a Mustang whose muscles twitched and shivered as it walked behind its rider. It looked like a bomb with four legs ready to explode at any moment. A long-handled tomahawk hung from his left hand. The large flat stone had been chiseled to a sharp blade and was as black as the Indian's eyes.

He looked at Captain Forrester, and their eyes locked. Suddenly Bill became calm. He knew how good a rider he was, and his skills with a saber were incomparable back at West Point. He felt his confidence begin to creep back into his mind, pushing aside his enemy, paranoia.

The rattle of the approaching wagon made everyone look. At the reins was the boy whom Tatter had sent off on an errand. In the bed of the buckboard were twenty watermelons on a layer of straw.

"Do you really think you can do this?" Levi whispered to his friend.

The captain grinned, but still, he didn't answer the question.

Finally, he turned his palms up and asked, "How can it get any easier than this?"

Both men mounted their horses, and the Crow Indian turned his icy gaze on Forrester. He was trying to unnerve him, but the captain was used to competing with his horse. It was the fastest animal he had seen since leaving Fort Leavenworth.

Forrester focused on his surroundings, forcing his breathing to steady and his heart to stop pounding between his ears. He sighed profoundly, letting all the tension release from his body. His hearing seemed magnified, and he heard his horse chew at its bit.

The white man and the Indian rode to the far end where the starter was standing. As the horses moved into position, he grabbed their reins. As the men tried to keep their animals calm, the starter glanced over his shoulder at Tatter. He let go, and a shot rang out—both horses burst forward with the power of a Baldwin locomotive. Horses' hooves hammered the earth as two clouds of dust corkscrewed behind the riders. Each man had six posts before him—three on either side. On the top of each post sat a watermelon the size of an average man's head. The posts were shoulder-high, so there was no mistaking the intention of the practice.

The Crow rider screamed a war cry. It was so shrill it spooked the captain's stallion, but to the dismay of the Sioux Indian, it burst into a neck-breaking sprint as they rushed toward the posts. The sun blazed down, baking everything, making the horses' flanks wet with sweat. Halfmoons showed under the arms of the riders, and their faces glistened with sweat.

Captain Forrester was a length and a half in front of the racing mustang. The horses' lungs sounded like steam engines as their riders pushed them to their limits. The wager was much more than a few beaver pelts and a long rifle. It was a battle between the skills of a white man and an Indian at a Native American game. The one who won would be bestowed with great honor. More than the captain ever imagined. Had he known, he might have done things differently.

Something made the riders shoot a glance at each other—again, their eyes met, and hostility flashed. The Sioux warrior reached out to grab at the captain, but his stallion shot forward and out of reach. Sun glinted off the captain's saber as he gracefully rode his horse with no hands, grabbing the sword with both fists as he swirled it over his head and cut all six watermelons in half like he was cutting hay with a scythe. Right behind him came the Sioux warrior. He, too, sliced all six melons in half, but he was two seconds behind the captain when they arrived at the end of the race.

A roar rose from their mountain men friends and dozens of others. The unusual wager spread through the crowd like wildfire, and soon a hundred spectators appeared. They gravitated to the most exciting event, like bees to honey. Levi whistled as Forrester pulled his horse up to a sliding halt and jumped off. His boots made little puffs of dirt.

Now the race was over, the Crow Indian looked like he had just taken a bite of a sour lemon. Just the same, he steered his horse toward his opponent and stopped. He dropped to the ground and pounded his fist over his heart—a sign of respect. The captain had proved they were near equals. If the warrior hadn't shouted and spooked the stallion, maybe the cards would have fallen another way —it was that close.

"If you could get ahold of your ego and listen for a change, you might just learn something," the losing Sioux's friend spat at his partner in their native tongue. "Now we're out twenty beaver pelts. Nearly the price of two guns."

Levi nodded, grinned, cleared his throat, and said in near disbelief, "You beat 'im!"

"Even a blind dog will find a bone once in a while," the captain replied, grinning like a mule.

Forrester popped a hand-rolled cigarette between his lips, which hung from the side of his mouth—he chuckled. Then they were all laughing, and all the mountain men were slapping the captain on the back. He suddenly realized he had just been admitted into the elite club of the Rocky Mountain men.

The story of the wager would find its way into the Indian gossip and spread across the mountains like wildfire. That and the new name of the captain would echo off the canyon walls. There were two new additions to the Rockies. Beaver and the captain would follow their six new friends to hunt buffalo and, later in the winter, trap beaver. Forrester would have a lot to learn, but he had Levi by his side, and he was unmatched as a trapper and had proved his skills as a sharpshooter. Now the true journey was about to begin.

"From now on, your name is Captain Blade," Rusty announced, "or just Blade for short. That *is* a wicked name if I ever heard one. I ain't never seen a man wield a long knife like that." He shook his head in admiration.

"Why don't you boys come and hang out with us here at the Rendezvous?" Dennis offered. "There's plenty of room. We're camped just on the other side of the event closest to the mountain trail."

"We always like to be ready to pull up stakes and leave if'n trouble starts, and it don't concern us," Angus said. "We tend to mind our own business, if'n you know what I mean. Now don't get me wrong. If some poor folks be in need, we be there to help, but we don't go lookin' for trouble. I just thought I might mention it. You being an army man and all."

"I don't like killin' any more than the next fellow," Blade replied. "I reckon my decision to be a military man like my father and my grandfather was mistaken, after all. I sure did waste a lot of time."

"I doubt there be nothin' better than an education," Rusty said. "I know how to read, but I only learned once I was a full-grown man. Most of us who live up in the mountains can't read a lick. We seldom get anything to read anyway other than summers like this. I have already bought all three newspapers available. I'll save 'em for when we have a boring night. The boys like for me to read to 'em by the fire."

"That'll do with the jaw waggin'," Syracuse Sam said. "I'm parched and could use a sip of whiskey. They have nothing but the best here at the Rendezvous. You best drink up while it's free, and we can because once we're back on the mountain, the best we can do is homemade corn or potato liquor."

Little by little, the crowd dispersed and moved on to other events. Levi, Blade, and their new friends moseyed around the event, checking out each competition. The atmosphere was almost like a carnival event where everybody was friendly and had a good time.

When they passed a dancing competition, Angus made everybody stop. He said, "Hold on right there now, boys. You know how I fancy a good dance. I was known as the *dancing king* back when I was a boy."

"Wait till you see old Angus cut up the floor," Rusty said to his two young friends.

It was strange for Rusty Steel to sidle up to people he didn't know. All five of his friends noticed, but nobody said anything about it. They all met him when he had come from ten years alone in the wilderness. After all these years, he had become comfortable with Dennis and his gang of misfits, but it was a surprise when he made friends with Levi and Blade. It was the last thing they expected of him. Usually, when he occasionally encountered white strangers on the mountain, he turned around and walked the other way because he wasn't interested in many relationships. He preferred to wander alone. But little by little, he came to confide in his five old friends, who all came to live on the same mountain.

"You're gonna love watching Angus clog," Rusty said.

Both Levi and Blade gave him a puzzled look.

"Hillbilly dancin' is what it is. Angus calls it buck dancin'."

Sure enough, the tall, gangly man with the long clumsy-looking legs walked up to the wooden floor provided for the contest. A fiddle, banjo, mandolin, and a harmonica worked out a tune, and old Angus's legs went to work like a pair of scissors. Each time his toe or heel hit the wood plank floor, it sounded like someone knocking on a door.

Refreshments were provided right there by the music. Many people paid little mind to the dancing but bobbed their heads to the catchy tunes provided by the band from the American Fur Trading Company.

7

WESTERN ROCKIES

Once the Rendezvous began to wind down, the mountain men were all business. Suddenly they all seemed to have a destination and were focused on the task. They loaded their mules with all the supplies they had bartered and the rest of their earnings they had in silver coins. It had been a grand winter, and the earnings proved it. They even had money left after their purchases and the new rifles. Rusty Steel even scored a spyglass—something he had wanted for years. It would give him an upper hand with a grizzly if he could see it far before it became aware he was there.

It would also go a long way to see Indians before they came into view with the naked eye. A man with a good spyglass could see for miles. It would become valuable, too, when they went hunting buffalo. It was wise to make sure some other Indian tribe didn't already claim the herd you decided to hunt. At times the buffalo numbered in the hundreds of thousands, so one could have a sizable hunting party on the other side of the herd and not know it. That was a situation that could provide potential danger. Indians didn't like sharing their herd with other tribes and especially not with white men with modern rifles.

The two newcomers to the life followed every detail they were given. Both men feared messing up and losing some of the dearly earned respect they had managed to acquire from these men who were now their peers. Still, the men seemed to have mutual respect and never asked another to do something they didn't want to. That was why this strange little gang of trappers and hunters of the wilderness stuck together for years. These scarce qualities in men were what gave Rusty confidence in his fellow man again. Now he felt at home with them as long as the visits to what he called civilization were limited to the Rendezvous, which in reality wasn't civilization at all.

It had been days—weeks since they arrived at the Rendezvous, and now both Levi and Blade were ready to leave the drinking and dancing behind for a glimpse of what was in store. They headed for Northern Utah and the Western Rockies. At first, the excitement of seeing the highest peaks made them nervous. Soon they realized they had a long and arduous trek to the mountain where these six gruff and shaggy men lived.

8

BLACKWATER CREEK

After weeks of walking and riding, they arrived at the mountain Dennis had discovered years ago. It was in a place between tribes where there was enough game for them to hunt and procure plenty of furs, but the hunting wasn't plentiful enough to support an Indian camp of a hundred or more. When Mountain Dennis discovered his slice of heaven all those years ago, he built his cabin and lived in solitude for several winters. He trapped and hunted but mainly traded with the Western Ute and Crow for food and whatever supplies he needed.

When a group of four hunters got stranded in a winter blizzard, their only refuge was his cabin. The winter was long, and they all became fast friends, and in the spring, they began to build two more cabins beside Dennis's. It resembled a small compound with a yard separating the three buildings. Together they built stables to keep the livestock from freezing in the harsh winters. They would spend the worst winter months inside, curing furs and repairing tools and traps. They each owned five or six traps. They were too heavy to carry more.

The compound was encircled with a zig-zag wooden fence with a gate on either side to access north and south trails. Each cabin had a small, covered porch on the front where they would enjoy the summer months and where fresh mountain breezes kept the heat at bay. The houses also gave them protection from Indian attacks that happened upon occasion. Some were in earnest, and others were in an attempt to see the white men's strength. But all three cabins had wooden shutters two inches thick with gun slats cut into each one and a three-inch oak door on the fronts. They were made of thick-hued logs that made it look like a small fort.

Since the group of mountain men never created problems and never poached the Indians' game or beaver, they lived in harmony with their environment. At least most of the time. Occasionally a Blackfoot or Sioux war party would decide they had seen enough settlers or white men wandering the mountains to rile them up and set them on the warpath. War was the Indian way, as most tribes were warriors and often traded captured men from other tribes to be used as slaves. This was not the white man's world with white men's rules. There it was the survival of the fittest.

Mountain men didn't come to the Rocky Mountains with visions of vast passages of land they could claim for their own. They were a long way from any unaware settlers. Rather than make war with most Indians, they preferred to live in comfortable peace and trade for bare essentials. They might build a cabin but knew the land wasn't theirs. The Indians said the land didn't belong to them—they belonged to the land. Most mountain men's boots soon wore out with such rugged terrain, so they usually adopted the moccasin from the local Indians or made their own. Eventually, the only eastern clothing they had left was what they could procure from the Rendezvous or trade with another passing mountain man.

Some believed they all came from the West, but these rugged men came from all walks of life—from wealthy businessmen who had had enough of city life to paupers who had no choice but to live such a torturous existence. Sometimes the occasional army officer would take a leave of absence, much like Captain Forrester, to make their fortunes in the Rocky Mountains. Few found riches, though, but they all found hardships. These difficult times would be traded for the chance to see snowcapped mountain peaks never seen by white men.

They were the true pathfinders named by the newspapers back east. Yet these men followed the paths the Indians made as they pursued game into the forests. Later, these same white men would hire on for trapping expeditions to lead the way. They knew the mountains like they knew themselves.

As they crossed the plains, it was hard for Levi to get a grasp on distances. He was usually very good at calculating how far away a landmark was, but on the Great Plains, he was lost. They had to cross this stretch of open country to get to the trail at the base of the Rocky Mountains. That was the way back to what these men had called home for many years. Now they had just added two new people to their sparse population.

In the open country, they rode their horses, leading the string of mules behind. They traveled at a leisurely pace. They were away from all the people and headed for their mountain homes' peace and quiet. The tops of trees swayed with the air, and white cotton-like clouds dotted the bright blue sky.

Suddenly Rusty stopped and sniffed—an out-of-place scent.

"Do ya smell that?" Rusty asked as he sniffed again—much like a bear.

Levi looked into the distance, couldn't see a thing, and replied, "All I smell is dirt."

"Exactly," Rusty shouted as he pulled out his new spyglass and peered into the far distance. "I can see the dust cloud from here."

He collapsed the telescope and slipped it into one of the large pockets on the side of his buckskin shirt. He kneeled, looked at the other men, and said, "Shush now while I listen."

Levi and Blade exchanged puzzled looks. Nobody made a sound. The other mountain men appeared to know what he was on about as Rusty put his ear to the ground.

"I can hear 'em coming, and they ain't all that far away," Rusty said. "I figure in a spell they'll be loud and clear."

"Who'll be loud and clear?" Levi asked.

"The buffalo stampede that's headed this way," Rusty said, but he spoke in a matter-of-fact tone void of fear.

Something told the two newcomers this wasn't something all that unusual. The mountain men all looked around to find the best place to take cover, but none seemed in a panic or hurry.

"Lookee over there, Rusty," Angus said. "See where it looks like there's a crack in the land?"

Rusty pulled out the spyglass again and said, "It's big enough to walk the horses and mules down. I reckon it's big enough to fit all the animals and us. It's like a thin crevice in the rock. If we can make it over there, we might be all right. How far you reckon it be?"

Rusty looked at Levi—he took a wild guess and said, "Ten minutes, maybe."

"That's a half-hour's ride at full gallop, partner," Rusty corrected him. "With the mules slowing us down, I reckon we'll be hard-pressed to make it before they be on us. Then again, we might just get lucky. I'd hate to lose the mules with all the supplies."

"What caused the herd to stampede?" Levi asked as he stared in the distance at the barely visible herd. He wondered what it would feel like when they felt their hooves hammer the ground by the hundreds of thousands.

"A poor shot at the herd's bull or maybe the Indians set them a-running," Rusty explained. "Sometimes they run herds of bison off cliffs, and then they skin 'em to make their teepees and lodges. They eat the meat and use the bones to make tools, fishhooks, and sewing needles. You name it, they use buffalo to make it. That's why they be touchy when we trespass on their property and kill their buffalo."

"I reckon they might have put that herd into a stampede to kill us," Angus said, using the flat of his hand to shade his eyes as he looked toward a massive killing machine. "They've done it to us before when they thought we were there to hunt their buffs. I reckon they believe we be poachers."

"But we're just passing through," Levi said as he strained his eyes to look into the distance.

"Whatever it is, we best stop waggin' our jaws and run for shelter,"

Syracuse Sam said. "This ain't gonna be pleasant, boys. It scares the dickens out of me every time it happens. Especially if we survive the stampede and have to face the Indians, I'd hate to be scalped again. The first time was bad enough."

"Scalped?" Levi asked, clearly shocked by the surprise. "You mean you've been scalped and lived to talk about it."

Sam grabbed the tail of his raccoon skin cap and pulled it off. It uncovered a mangled skull full of scar tissue from a couple of inches above the brow to the back of his head. He had just enough hair left in the back to make a small ponytail.

"Ain't ya never seen a man scalped before?" Sam asked and laughed at the green color both the new men's faces had taken.

"Yee-ha!" Rusty yelled as he gigged his horse, and they all began to run for cover.

As they raced for shelter, Levi couldn't help but glance off his shoulder every few seconds to see if the buffalo were in sight yet. Now he could feel the nervousness of the men and the horses. They didn't have to push the horses. They seemed to know what was coming. That was not the case with the mules.

First, he saw a massive dust cloud that rose so high it blocked out part of the sky. Dirt and brush swirled in the air as the vast bison herd rushed toward the mountain men. At first, they could hear a distant rumbling. Then as the herd came closer, the ground began to quake in their path. It felt like an earthquake when they funneled into the valley, where the white men raced for cover.

Rusty led the way, and Dennis took up the drag to ensure none of the mules were lost. He cracked a whip at the end of the string urging the animals to move forward as fast as they could. Now the mules sensed the urgency; their eyes spread wide as some of their horses squealed, and others groaned.

Levi and Blade could see it would be a close call. Dennis was lashing at the rumps of the mules as their time was quickly running out. Suddenly the refuge was right in front of them. Rusty was the first to bump his horse down to a trot and entered the crevice in the ground. A water runoff had made it in the rainy season. Now it was deep and dry and provided plenty of room for all of them.

No sooner did the last mule enter the shelter than thousands of buffalo were on them. The men ducked down against the near wall of the gorge in case one of the buffalo stumbled in and landed on top of them. The noise drowned out every other sound—it was almost maddening. It seemed to last forever. Brown curly fur floated in the air as they passed. Then, just as suddenly as it started, it was over.

That night the only thing they talked about was the buffalo stampede. Apparently, it started on its own as no Indians followed the herd, nor did they run off cliffs, but the raw adrenaline stayed with them as they detailed every moment. For Rusty Steel and his friends, it was just another experience and another day in the wilderness.

They couldn't make camp there on the plains because everything was trampled flat. They rode for higher ground where they could collect enough wood to make a fire to keep the night chill off, even though it was summer. As the older mountain men recounted their experiences with herds of bison, the young men listened in awe. They clung to their every word.

The next day they moved on again, headed for the mountains in the distance. Levi felt he could nearly reach out and grab them with his hand. Once again, the distances on the plains he found tricky. By this time, Blade had become a changed man. He had shed his army responsibilities, been given a nickname, and had a new goal. Levi and Blade had no particular destination in mind. They just wanted to see the Rocky Mountains before the settlers began to populate the valleys below.

After ten days of hard travel, they climbed high into the mountains and headed for their new friends' cabins. Suddenly they were walking into a clearing where the cabins were located. They herded the cattle into the corral and began to unload the supplies. Everybody was busy tending to the animals and hardly uttered a word. The whole time Levi and Blade looked at their surroundings with eyes as big as does'.

The place was just like Levi had pictured it would be from the stories they had told around the fire. It was still summer, and the days were long and warm. He imagined hunting would be excellent in such dense forests. Giant trees towered over the men as the mules brayed and blew in protest to the long trek.

Once the animals were unloaded, brushed down, fed, and watered, the men turned their attention to themselves. Dennis and Rusty lived in one cabin, and Pete and Angus shared a house along with his Crow wife. She stayed there often. When she got tired of his white ways, she moseyed back to her family for a month or two. It was common for mountain men to take Indian wives. They were the women who had the most in common with them.

"Levi, you can stay with me, and Dennis and Blade can bunk with Yosemite Bob," Rusty said.

"First things first," Angus said as he began to make something to eat. "Now that we're home, we can have a proper meal."

There were buffalo steaks, frying-pan biscuits, strips of salted bacon, and a boiling pot of black beans in an hour. The aroma of freshly perked coffee floated on puffs of air, mixing with the smell of pine trees. Everybody seemed to be talking at once until the meal was ready, and then the only sound was spoons and knives scraping against tin pie pans.

Angus sliced sugar off a solid cone and into his cup of coffee. They passed the dark brown sugar around and laced the coffee with a dash of corn liquor. Dennis had built a still years before and supplied them with a taste of moonshine when the moment was right. None of them drank in excess except in the Rendezvous. There it was, the order of the day, and most of the mountain men attending were so drunk by the end of the event they had gambled away all their earnings and hardly knew where they were. Some took days to sober up, but Rusty and his friends could hold their liquor and knew when to stop.

Luckily none of them were foolish enough to gamble away their hard-earned pelts and furs. They spent the entire winter at the task of trapping, shooting, skinning, and curing the skins into something so soft and supple they got the top price.

Many a man had gotten drunk, offended the wrong mountain man, and ended up in a shallow grave. These people were nearly as wild as the Indians they portrayed their lives after. They only had their word and their wits to survive in a hostile environment.

The question suddenly hit Levi. Why did these men do what they did and live as they did? And why did he feel so drawn to them and their way of life? He turned to look at the captain, but he still saw the indecision on his face. Johnson imagined it would be difficult for Bill to deal with the change in life, especially since he had planned his entire adulthood for the military. Now he suddenly found fate had rather ruthlessly thrown him in a new and unexpected direction. For him, the change may prove difficult, while for Levi, it would be as easy as falling off a log.

Levi had lived in Southwest Indiana much in the same manner. His family had a simple cabin, and they trapped and hunted for food and furs. The only difference was here, they had to deal with Indians —both friendly and hostile. That and the animals were as dangerous as the harsh Blackfeet, if not more. Then there were the mountains and winter blizzards with snow so deep the only way to travel was with snowshoes. He could hardly wait.

As they sat on Rusty's porch, they sipped at their coffee as he spied Levi over the brim of his tin cup. He smiled, and it reached his eyes. Something about this young man reminded him of someone far back in his past. He had yet to put his finger on who that was, though. There was something as familiar as apple pie. That was what drew the customarily reserved man who mixed with very few people.

Now he saw some potential. His friends were mountain men of the highest category and had lived in the Rockies for many years. Maybe deep inside, it was a simple curiosity to see if the two young wannabe mountain men had the stuff it took not only to survive— because of that, he had little doubt about their skills—but to succeed in ways other men hadn't. He thought that maybe one of the two had the stuff it took—perhaps even both. They certainly did have a wagonload of determination. That was something he found rare in the young men he met in the meet.

Every year the Rendezvous brought more and more people. Initially, they were only mountain men and Indians, much like Rusty. In the later years, hawkers, card sharps, and even soiled doves found their way to the event. The more people that came, the longer it seemed to last, year after year. This year he had even seen what he had to imagine to be tourists. Their fancy clothing didn't match anything anyone else wore at the Rendezvous. He saw something in Levi and Blade that he had seen years ago in himself and even Dennis and Angus, who had been in the mountains the longest.

"Whatcha think of our little settlement here in the middle of the wilderness, Beaver?" Rusty asked as he stared at the two young men.

"I'd hardly call this a settlement," Levi said. "There's only three cabins. I'd say it's more like a compound. It sure feels safer than it did back in the forest afoot."

Angus walked out the door and slipped his new rifle over his shoulder. He hung a waterskin around his neck and turned to go.

"Do you think she'll still be waitin' on ya?" Rusty laughed. "He's gonna see if his Crow wife is still angry with him and is ready to return to the cabin for a spell."

"He's really married to a Crow Indian?" Levi asked.

"He's been married to three Crow, and he had a Pawnee wife, too," Dennis said. He could hardly keep a straight face.

Angus stood there, his eyes shooting daggers at his friends, Dennis and Rusty. They always gave him a hard time about his wives. He was in a hurry because sometimes he stayed away too long, and when he got back, they divorced him and married some young brave. It was tricky business keeping an Indian wife happy and earning a living as a trapper and hunter.

"Go on then—get," Rusty spat. "You know you can't wait." His laugh was full and loud.

"Why do I feel like you two are always hackin' on me for no good reason? I figure you two be jealous is what you are. Neither of you had more than one wife, and they were white women. Only a real mountain man marries into the tribes."

Angry, Angus turned on his heels and stormed off. As soon as he hit the tree line, he disappeared, despite the sun slanting through the trees like rain. The brush and forest only allowed a fraction of the rays to penetrate. He vanished almost immediately.

Levi briefly wondered what it was going to be like wandering through this forest on his own. He preferred to hunt by himself, although it was handy to have another set of hands when trapping. Then they could carry another five or six traps. But hunting was something almost religious for Levi Beaver Johnson. He liked it to be personal and between him and his prey. Most of the time, he was the victor, and he made his kill. Here he believed it wouldn't be so cut and dry. If you missed a shot on a grizzly bear, you only made it angrier.

Or if you ran across a mother and her cubs, you would be guaranteed a battle to the death. Nothing was more dangerous than a grizzly mother protecting her litter of cubs. Levi had experienced the same thing with black bears back in Indiana, but he knew the bears in the Rockies were famous for their size and aggression.

Rusty pulled a twist of tobacco from his pocket, cut a plug off with his knife, and popped it into his mouth, making his cheek puff out. He offered the twist to Levi and Blade, and they filled their ceramic pipes. They had bought them in the trading post. Almost all the mountain men they saw smoked ceramic pipes and bought tobacco twists. They could be chewed or smoked. They stocked up heavily on tobacco and coffee. Not only for them to enjoy but to trade with the local Indians. They were two products cherished by one and all in the mountains.

"The boys and me got to tend to our cabins. You two can go off and see if you can scare up some meat," Rusty said. "A buffalo or a couple of elk would do just fine."

9

BEES TO BEARS

The following morning, Levi and Blade were up and ready to venture out into the woods. They had a job to do, and it wouldn't look good if they failed. Levi took his Hawken long gun, and Captain Blade his Colt carbine six-shot rifle. They each carried a brace of pistols for defense. The rifles were for hunting.

They had decided to go on foot to get a better look at the lay of the land. They had two pack mules in tow to carry their kills back home. The first mule held provisions for a few days, so they weren't in any hurry. Levi was a first-class tracker, so even though he was in unknown territory, he had no problem backtracking on his own trail to find his way back to the cabins.

Captain Blade didn't have these skills, and it left him feeling uneasy. It would be essential for him to become a good tracker and quick. He wasn't in the army where he could hire Indian scouts to keep him out of trouble. If he got separated from Levi, he'd never find his way back to the little hollow and the three cabins in the middle of the dense forest.

"I reckon now is as good a time as any to start to learn how to track, Beaver. I just realized if I get separated from you, I don't know where I'm at."

Honeybees buzzed across the trail, stopping to take pollen from the abundance of flowers. Small swarms dashed around in the air, and all flew down the path to take their nectar to their hive and start the process again.

"Don't worry, pard," Levi chuckled. "I don't know where I'm at either, but I can always find our way back from where we came."

The captain watched as Levi traveled through the forest and hardly made a sound. He tried to step in his footsteps like he had shown him before. He felt clumsy and couldn't help but make noise. Every once in a while, Levi glanced over his shoulder to ensure his buddy was close. He shot him the occasional dirty glance for making too much noise.

"If you ramble through the forest like a bull, you're gonna scare off all the elk," Levi said. "Not to mention alert any Indians who might be out there hunting, too. Remember, we ain't the only ones out here. We wanna try to go unperceived, Captain. With the noise we're makin', we might as well have brought the horses."

Captain Blade wasn't accustomed to being criticized by men who were under him. Suddenly he had to remind himself he wasn't in charge anymore. It was something he wasn't used to, and he instantly didn't like it. For some reason, it rubbed against his grain. He had to remind himself where he was and who he was with now. He obviously wasn't the one in charge anymore, and he was way out of his depth in knowledge of surviving his current environment.

He gave Levi a sharp glance, but his friend just snickered. He knew how hard it must be for an ex-West Point officer to eat humble pie in an environment he wasn't suited for. He was like a fish out of water in the woods. At least Levi knew if they had a scrap, he was a better fighter against other men than he was or even wanted to be. Levi wasn't that kind of man. He only killed when forced, and the three Indians he shot in the back still hung heavy on his mind. He wondered if the captain felt the same or had any idea of how he thought about the incident. No, Levi Beaver Johnson was a tracker, trapper, and hunter, but he wasn't a killer. Not like his friend Blade was.

They carefully made their way through the forest, moving from one shadowy place to another, always trying to leave their images exposed for as short a time as possible. Animals looked for movement. Sometimes they would look right at Levi but couldn't see him because he sat as still as a stone. That was when he took his shot and always ensured it was a well-placed bullet. He disapproved of an animal needlessly suffering any more than necessary.

Some people back in Indiana felt Levi was too affable a man to live in the Rocky Mountains. Most of his cousins thought he was crazy to leave a safe home. He always had plenty of work and brought in more kills than any other hunter in the southwestern part of the state. Still, everybody but his pa was surprised when he left. They thought he would talk about going until the urge passed, and then he would stay back where he was born and raised. Some men were born fiddle-footed, though. Levi figured all mountain men suffered this ailment. They just couldn't stay put.

Beaver looked up and saw several beehives hanging from the trees overhead. It gave him pause as he looked around for animals that loved honey. He proceeded slowly and with extreme caution.

When Blade saw the track, he couldn't believe its size. It looked like a bear track, but it was as big around as his head. He opened his mouth to speak and pointed at the ground, but no words came out. In his mind's eye, he imagined how big an animal had to be to leave a paw mark like that.

"Beaver," Blade finally whispered the words. "Look at that."

Levi shot a glance over his shoulder and stopped in his tracks. He put his finger to his lips and squatted. Captain Blade followed suit. His heart was pounding so hard he was sure Levi could hear it. For all appearances, Beaver maintained calm and relaxed like he was hunting for squirrels or rabbits. The problem with the animal somewhere near them was that it was maybe fifteen hundred pounds. The captain looked at Levi's rifle, which suddenly seemed smaller than when he bought it. Then, he had thought it was enormous and too heavy to carry. Now, he wondered if it would be big enough.

He held his Colt carbine in white-knuckled fists as he followed

Levi's eyes, searching for signs of the animal that left the footprint. Then he heard the sound every hunter dreaded. It was the crying sound of two baby cubs. Right after they heard them, they saw them tumble onto the trail as they played, brother and sister. Behind them lumbered a heavy mother grizzly bear. She was a monster. Until now, she showed no signs of being aware the white hunters were nearby.

When Levi looked down at his new rifle, it suddenly looked like a pop gun a child would use. He made a note to remember to buy the biggest gun money could buy next time he had the opportunity. That is, if they didn't perish that very day.

The captain was sure the bear could hear him breathe—maybe even hear his heartbeat as it hammered in his chest. Perspiration glistened on his face, and beads of sweat streamed down his back. When he looked over at Levi, he seemed as still as the tree he hid behind. He didn't even appear to be breathing. Neither man moved. One was focused on the bear, watching everything it did and taking note of its habits. The other was in an environment that wasn't his, and he knew it. He knew they would perish before the monster bear standing not twenty yards from where they hid, if left up to him.

Finally, the two cubs ran down the trail away from the hidden hunters. The mother turned to go, but then she stopped for a moment and stood on her hind legs—sniffing the air as if she felt the presence of the two humans. She grunted, then turned and ran after her babies.

Blade went to speak, but Levi held up his hand to stop him. He waited patiently for over an hour. Blade supposed he was waiting to see if the mother bear returned or not. He had no idea what was happening since Beaver wouldn't allow him to talk. He suddenly realized what it was like when he gave his soldiers orders they couldn't understand but were expected to follow anyway.

When the male grizzly bear roared, it could be heard all over the forest. As soon as it made its presence known, small animals scurried through the woods, rustling bushes all around them. Even the birds took flight after the piercing growl. As the brown furry monster lumbered into view, it sniffed at the ground where the mother bear and the cubs had been. It looked like he may be after one of her cubs. Levi saw his intentions and frowned.

As the bear inspected the place where the cubs were, Levi felt a change in the direction of the breeze. He pulled a tuft of grass and let it fall. Now they were upwind of the bear. The wind had rolled 180 degrees. Instantly, the bear's nose shot up in the air and took a deep whiff. Its eyes searched before it until Levi's and the bear's met. The massive animal roared again. This time it made hackles stand on the captain's neck. He raised his carbine just as Levi pulled the trigger.

The blast was much louder than Blade had expected. Levi hadn't been ready for the recoil—it nearly broke his shoulder. He thanked his lucky stars he had loaded it for buffalo. The bear was almost as big as the bull they had seen on the way up the mountains. When the bullet hit its left eye, it exploded—blood covered its face instantly. It made a last-ditch effort to roar at its assailant, but halfway through, it rocked on its heels and fell over backward with a loud thud. It was a perfect shot. Levi opened the chamber and blew down the barrel—gray smoke puffed out the end.

Levi stood and slowly moved toward the downed grizzly. The captain carefully followed. Neither one was quite sure it was really dead, even with the perfect headshot. It had seemed invincible.

"I wonder if'n the boys like bear meat?" Levi asked. He finally sighed and smiled.

"I've never had the pleasure," Blade replied.

As the adrenaline surge passed, the captain suddenly felt very tired. It was the same feeling he had felt in the past in combat.

"I've never eaten grizzly bear, either. We've got some hard work to do, but let's have a smoke first and ponder on what just happened."

Levi reloaded his rifle, leaned it against a tree, and then sat at the base. He grinned as he pulled out his tobacco twist and filled a cigarette paper. He pulled out a wooden match from the boxes he had bought at the Rendezvous. He scratched the head on his pistol's hammer, and it burst into a yellow-blue flame with the smell of sulfur. He looked at his handiwork with his smoke dangling from his lips. He blew out a cloud of smoke and chuckled. When he looked at his friend, he was sound asleep. He sat with his head against the massive tree trunk and snored lightly.

Levi thought it strange how things worked out in the end. He remembered back the first time he had seen the captain ride into Fort Scott with his white stallion and his fancy cavalry hat slapped up on one side. He made quite a picture. Back then, Johnson was no more than an unemployed wannabe scout. It was funny how the tides had turned, and now the captain found himself entirely out of his element. Sure, he was hell on wheels when in a scrap, but he lacked some basic knowledge to live in such an environment.

Johnson wondered how long the captain would make it. Would he give it up, turn, and run with his tail between his legs? Or would he buck up and focus on learning how to survive in the wilderness? Many men lost their lives in the process. Levi could thank his lucky stars he had grown up in such an environment. He did not doubt that he was going to make a first-class mountain man. Hopefully, he could help his friend learn what he needed before he got frustrated and gave up—or killed in the process.

Levi remembered how he had planned to travel to the Pacific Ocean with the captain. Now their plans had all literally gone up in smoke, and they found themselves somewhere other than their intended destination.

The bear's fur ruffled in the breeze. The wind had shifted yet again; now they were downwind to the bear, and it stank. The smell was of musty fur and death. The acrid odor of blood lingered in the air. The men knew the job that lay ahead. It was going to be challenging to skin such a large animal.

"How are we going to gut and skin him, Beaver?" Captain Blade asked as he blinked his eyes open. "I doubt the two of us could budge him an inch."

"Grab that rope, tie it around its legs, and throw it over that limb. We can use the mules to pull it up and tie it to the tree. Then we can gut and skin it while it's hanging. But don't you worry. It's still gonna be a heck of a job."

Once they had it hanging from the large tree, they stood back and proudly admired their prize. They hobbled the mules and let them graze while they began slaughtering the bear.

"I guess we can spend the night here and ride back tomorrow, can't we?" the captain asked.

"We'll spend the night somewhere, but it won't be here with this carcass lying on the ground. Every wolf, coyote, and jackal will be snooping around fightin' over the remains. When they're done, there won't be nothin' left but bones."

Levi pulled his hatchet from the tools on the mule and used it to remove the bear's claws. He had heard Rusty say the Indians thought they were big medicine, so he figured he would make a necklace. The next Indians he ran into would know he was dangerous if he could kill a giant grizzly bear.

When they were done, they left the scene of the killing behind for the scavengers, worms, and flies. Even before they were finished gutting the animal, they saw a dozen vultures circling in the sky above them—a number of crows cawed from high in the tree's limbs. A feast was at hand, and the first arrivers would get most of the spoils.

They traveled a few miles back toward the cabins without mishap. All the meat was on salt, and the large skin was rolled up and packed on the back of a mule. The hunting expedition, which had been expected to last several days, turned out to be a night out and back the next day. For amateurs, Levi figured they were doing pretty danged good.

They built a small fire to keep off the evening chill and marveled at their accomplishment that day.

"How's it feel to bag your first bear?" Levi asked.

"I didn't shoot it—you did," the captain replied. "If our lives depended on me, I believe we would be dead right now. There were no classes on how to kill grizzly bears at West Point. I am afraid I am out of my league here in the wilderness."

"But are ya willin' to learn?" Levi asked.

"If you're willing to teach me. Hopefully, I will learn enough before our host, Mr. Steel, throws me out for being worthless."

"Oh, I figure you have another value for 'im," Levi replied. "You were the soldier that beat the Sioux Indian at the Rendezvous competition."

"Do you think the story would make it all the way up here to the mountains?" the captain asked.

"Rusty and Dennis both said the Indian gossip traveled as quick as spit and that most every Indian on the mountain would know you were the fella with the long knife. If I'm not mistaken, you, my friend, are insurance against an Indian attack."

"Do you really think so?"

"I'm pretty sure of it," Levi replied. "I saw how they looked at ya before you had a go at that Sioux brave. Before that, all they saw was another army officer trying to make a name for himself, and it didn't work out. They don't exactly hide their feelings, now, do they? The way they looked at you after you sliced those six watermelons off like they were enemy heads—they all had to take a second look. Especially Rusty. I don't know why he's taken a shinin' to us, but I sure am glad he has."

"I'm looking forward to seeing their faces when we come back with this grizzly bear. I doubt they thought we would be back tomorrow."

"Don't worry, pard. They'll probably just send us right back out to hunt some more. Winters are long and will be a mite more enjoyable with good meals. There's eight of us now, so we have our work cut out for us."

10

SIOUX WARRIOR

Despite orders from his chief, the warrior brave, Black Bear, ignored his elders and set off to find the bluecoat that shamed him at the Rendezvous. He knew he could never live it down. Of course, the story had spread far and wide in the local gossip. The army soldier had songs made of his skills while his peers shunned the Sioux warrior for his defeat.

Even though it was against the Rendezvous rules, Black Bear had made this a personal vendetta. He knew what was expected of him, but he couldn't help himself. He had to have revenge, even if it meant he would be banished from the tribe. He couldn't face his fellow warrior braves as it was. Even if he died by the captain's long knife, it would be better than living in shame, isolated from his family, people, and tribe.

He had left the Rendezvous with his friends, but they were all sick from drinking the white man's whiskey. He left them in disgust. The fur traders poisoned them with their spirits and made them foolish, trading their furs below the market price or gambling their pelts away. After the competition, he was angry with the world. He needed somebody to blame for his failure, but there was no one. The only way to save his honor was to kill the captain with his tomahawk, and he had to do it in front of the other white men. That way, he knew everyone in the mountains and valleys would hear that Black Bear had gotten his revenge and proved he was the better man.

At first, he had considered ambushing the captain, but then he would have no witnesses. This revenge was more about his ego than the death of his enemy—or even himself. He could only live with the shame if the white man died by his black stone blade. So, he turned back, leaving his fellow warriors to go home alone, and he looked for the tracks of Rusty Steel and his string of mules. Anybody could follow his tracks.

He was one of the most successful trappers in the mountains. This year Rusty and his partners brought nearly seven hundred pelts to the Rendezvous. This left them with plenty of money to make their cabins a little more comfortable on those winter nights when the temperatures dropped to twenty below zero. Everybody knew Rusty Steel was a crafty mountain man, but they also knew he was honest. That was why he was so successful.

Black Bear instantly realized killing one of Rusty Steel's friends would mean he would have to kill him too. But then he would have his five friends shoot him to pieces. It was true—he had known all along but hadn't confronted the end in his mind. He truly believed that he would kill the soldier simply because he was a Sioux warrior, and no white soldier without a gun was a match for such a foe. What happened at the contest was some sort of magic or a trick.

This time they would be chopping off human heads and not watermelons. There would be no more possibility of a trick because he would catch them off guard with all the mountain men present. All he had to do was find their cabins. He had heard they lived in a small fortress which was hard to approach. That meant that Black Bear would have to catch the captain coming or leaving, and he had to be quick. Faster than his young friend with the rifle. If he wasn't careful, he could kill him before he got his revenge. He knew he had to forfeit his life due to his actions. But now he could proudly pass over to the spirit world knowing he had made a wrong right. In the end, the elders would make songs of his actions, and they wouldn't be his actions at the Rendezvous—they would be those at the cabins.

He came onto the clearing so suddenly he nearly stumbled into sight. There was no sign of the group of buildings until he was right on top of them. A sufficient field of fire was cleared around the three heavy timber cabins and a split-log zigzag fence. He even saw Rusty Steel and Angus, who was married to the Crow woman, sitting on the porch but no sign of the two newcomers everyone was talking about.

He waited until dark, then carefully cut branches and bushes and made himself a suitable blind he could observe them from and not allow them to see him. He would wait there as long as it took. He had water and some hard tack. Once he arrived, it wouldn't matter anymore anyway. Everything would be over then. He would be in the spirit world with his father.

This time it would be different. There would be no magic wooden posts and no magic watermelons. There would be no tricks or traps. There would be reliable witnesses, even if it was Rusty Steel. Everybody knew he never broke his word or lied.

He could smell the white soldier. He wore the same smell on their first encounter. The second mountain man smelt wild, like nature. His scent was harder to identify. He smelled much like an Indian.

Levi rode point towing the two mules, and Blade rode drag, making sure they kept up a reasonable pace. They weren't in a hurry, but a mountain lion or another hungry bear could smell bear meat and blood from a long distance. You always had to keep your eyes peeled in the wilderness, or you could have your life snatched away in a single heartbeat. One moment you were there and the next, you were gone.

After the bear, the captain's eyes shot everywhere, constantly vigilant for all sorts of dangers. Not only Indians but grizzly bears, like the one they just killed, ready to charge them. Not to mention snakes, black bears, leopards, and who know how many bugs could make you sick if not kill you, too, with the slightest warning.

Levi found it strange the simple things he had to teach the captain. He didn't even know what poison ivy or poison oak was. He lacked the knowledge of the most basic dangers everywhere along the mountainous trails. Poison ivy would make you miserable, and poison oak could cause boils and get infected. Rattlesnakes snuck into your boots during the night because it's warm. Tarantula climbed into your bedroll, so it, too, would be like toast. None of these things the captain knew about.

There were as many small critters that could kill you in the Rockies as there were large ones. Still, the king of them all was a buffalo bull: that and a male grizzly. Levi had shot the first effectively, dropping him in his tracks. It had been another perfect shot.

Levi hadn't missed the sour look on the Sioux warrior's face after the loss at the Rendezvous. He had kept a close eye on him before and after the event in case he got violent. He sure was mighty embarrassed with his fellow warriors making fun of him and everybody cheering for the captain and slapping him on the back. He was the event hero. He had gotten praise from all present.

"Did you see the face on that Sioux warrior you beat in the competition in the Rendezvous?" Levi asked his friend.

"I thought Rusty said it was all fun and games back at the reunion," the captain said. "He told me nobody got out of line, or they wouldn't be allowed to return."

"Maybe that Sioux warrior don't intend to return to the reunion," Levi said. "Maybe he was so shamed before his peers that he ain't gonna let that defeat go."

"You seem to be picking at straws, buddy," Bill said. "As far as I could see, it just looked like a bit of fun. Everybody was laughing and having a good time. Is that old friend of yours, paranoia, eating at your brain again?"

"That Sioux Indian you bested wasn't laughing," Levi replied. "You weren't paying attention, but I kept an eye on 'im just the same, and he was far from happy."

"You worry too much, my friend," the captain said. "Just think about how the boys will react when we come into camp with a seven-foot grizzly bear skin and meat for a month."

"I wonder why Rusty and Dennis didn't say anything about that Indian? They must have seen the same thing in his eyes that I did."

"Maybe they didn't see anything in his eyes because there wasn't anything there." Captain Blade smiled. "You're always seeing ghosts when they don't exist. I believe Rusty Steel would have mentioned it to us if it was a threat, don't you?"

"Well, I don't know," Levi said. "You could be right, but if you're wrong, we could get ambushed."

"According to Rusty and Dennis, he would be even more dishonored. They said the Indians put a lot of faith in honor and their word. Just like the mountain men. Not like some white people we've met along the trail!"

"Yeah, I reckon you're right, Bill. I was always careful when hunting back home in Indiana and never got myself into a bind. Since I've headed west, we seem to run into problems everywhere we go. Maybe I'm just getting a case of the quick-jumps."

The captain looked around and asked, "Are you sure this was the way we came?"

"I'm sure it ain't the way we came. Never go back the same way you came if you could find an alternate route. It's safer that way."

"There you go again," the captain said. "Paranoia will give you a heart attack before you're thirty if you keep worrying all the time."

"Maybe you're right. It's become a habit of mine ever since a mountain lion tracked me with the intention of eating me when I was a boy. The cat chased me across a river and all the way home. Lucky for me, he didn't attack, or I wouldn't be here now. The next day I went out with my pa and killed it. Ever since, I've kept my guard up when in the wilderness. You might consider listenin' to me, Captain. What could it hurt?"

"I'll tell ya what," Captain Blade said. "I'll try to be a little more careful if you try to relax a tad. You're as bad as my old lieutenant, James Harbin. He was nervous all the time. At least until a battle started, then he was the calmest of all my men. I never get scared for myself when going into battle. Most of my concern is for my soldiers.

This made him think back on the soldiers he had lost to the Comanche war party. It left a bad taste in his mouth, knowing he should have learned how to keep them from being killed. No matter from what side he looked at it, he couldn't see how, though. By all rights, they should have all perished by the Comanche. If they hadn't tricked them, they would be dead.

Even though he tried to avoid it, Levi's concerns were contagious, and a worm began to eat at the captain's stomach. He looked all around them, but the dense vegetation hampered visibility. There were dozens of places for an ambush to be placed.

"Now you got me getting paranoid," Captain Blade spat. "Stop it with the worrying. Now you got me looking all around for danger."

"Maybe that's a good state of mind to take until you learn more about the wilderness."

They rode on in silence, each man with his own thoughts. Levi was still concerned about the Sioux warrior, and Blade still wasn't convinced he had made the right choice when he cut his soldiers loose and sent in his resignation. Then it struck him. Maybe he was a coward after all. Perhaps he should have returned with his men to face the music.

He had no doubts about what would await him did he make such a decision. Going back, he would face inevitable reprimand and demotion if not being drummed out of the cavalry altogether. He had been proud of himself on his big white horse and fancy hat. Now he wondered who the fool was. Maybe he was just fooling himself, thinking he could escape what had happened. Now he felt small and defeated again. He had no idea if he did the right thing or not. The captain would have to wait to find out.

11

THE UNEXPECTED

"Pass that jug of corn liquor over here, ya stingy old cuss," Angus said. He held up his coffee cup while Rusty poured a smidgen into the steaming java.

"You surprised me, Rusty," Angus said. "I never took you for the type to allow a couple of strangers come home with ya. The other boys are as puzzled as I am. You have never been the friendliest type with folks you don't know."

"To be honest, I don't even know why I let 'em come along, either. If it don't work out, it's gonna be a long winter, but I've got faith in that young fella Levi. I let the captain come along just because they're friends, but I doubt he'll last. He don't seem the type to survive in the mountains. He needs an army behind him to be somebody."

"Like you said, it's gonna be a long winter," Angus said. "I'm lucky my Crow wife still has feelings for me. It's the darndest thing that. I always worry she'll drop me when I disappear for a month or so, but up till now, she's always waitin' for me. She told me she'll be along later today."

Rusty looked at his tall, gangly friend and wondered what the Indian women saw in him. They hardly gave him and Dennis the time of day, when ugly old Angus had to beat them off with a stick.

He'd had had so many girlfriends and wives over the years that he wondered how he kept count. Maybe it was his dancing skills.

The fact that there weren't any white women in the mountains wasn't lost on the mountain men. If they could find the right kind of white woman, they might consider taking a wife. It would make the long cold winters more entertaining, and it would be nice to have somebody to keep them warm. But neither man was the Indian-marrying type. They found living with the Crow was too different than what they were used to. Dennis had been married and even had children, but he lost them all to smallpox.

Rusty's life had been full of violence as a child, and then aboard the paddleboat, there wasn't any time for such frivolous things. Seeing the *Dragon Queen* burn and sink there along the riverbank had left him fed up with travelers, thieves, and hustlers. He had spent his first ten years in self-imposed isolation, alone other than the rare visit to his Crow friend. Since he moved in with the hunter and trappers here in the Rockies, he had all the company he needed.

It was hard to miss something you never had in the first place. Dennis had different feelings. He felt the Good Lord had given him one family, which was enough for a lifetime. He hoped he would see them when his day came to pass onto the other side.

"How long did Levi say he might be out hunting for winter meat?" Angus asked.

"Oh, I reckon he won't be too quick," Rusty said. "He's gonna have to get his bearings straight first. I figure they'll be back this week."

Rusty sniffed the air and made a face. "Don't look now, but we got company."

"Are the boys back already?" Angus asked as he looked up the trail leading to the mountains.

"It ain't the boys unless they've taken to covering their bodies with bear fat. I reckon we got some Indian spying on us."

Angus didn't immediately move but took his time inconspicuously looking around. His eyes caught a slight movement in his peripheral vision.

"I reckon you're right, pard," Angus whispered. He picked up a stick and acted like he was scratching in the dirt when he was really drawing a little map to show Rusty where he thought the Indian was.

Rusty just nodded and said, "I reckon it'll be that Sioux brave the captain bested back at the Rendezvous. Whatcha wanna do with 'im, Angus? Should we sneak up on 'im and take 'im captive, or should we let him wait it out and let things take their own course? It don't look like he's planning an ambush. Not so close to the cabins. I reckon he's here to call 'im out. You know I ain't one to mess with fate. Let's see how it plays out. I got my new Colt carbine right here if'n the Sioux warrior gets strappy with us, but I doubt that be his plan."

"He could be on a suicide mission," Angus said. "You know how them braves be once they're embarrassed. Some would rather die than admit defeat."

"I reckon he'll have a long wait unless Levi gets lucky and finds a pair of elk large enough to feed us. We have eight mouths to feed now, so we're gonna need much more food than last year."

They heard the clomping of horses' hooves before they saw the two hunters. Both men harumphed when they watched them enter the clearing with their pack mules weighed down. The grizzly skin was sitting right there on top of the first mule; all rolled up.

"Well, I'll be a son-of-a-gun," Angus said. "The young hunter bagged 'im a grizzly bear, and it looks like a sizable one too."

"Don't forget about that Indian waitin' out there," Rusty whispered.

He figured the Indian would have his eyes on the riders now that they had arrived. So, he took the chance to wrap his hands around his new carbine and lay it across his lap. The rest of the boys tended to their chores and were out gathering firewood for the winter.

Rusty and Angus stayed behind to keep an eye on all the goods they bought at the Rendezvous. It wouldn't be the first time a couple of thieves followed a few successful trappers home to steal what they earned. Men who didn't like working hard to make a living stole what was not theirs to avoid the labor.

The man hiding in the bushes wasn't a thief, though. If he was, he was terrible at his job. He should have known a mountain man could smell him just like he could smell the soap that many white men used. Your sense of smell was important when you lived in such a dense forest. An odor could carry a long way when your eyes couldn't see more than twenty feet into the foliage.

Rusty took his eyes away from where he expected the Sioux to be. He glanced at Levi and the captain. Forrester's face showed his lack of concern. Johnson's showed something totally different. He smelled the Indian too. Steel's gut feeling about the young man had been spot-on. He was brave, an excellent shot, and an impressive tracker, and he wasn't a fool—something he still couldn't say about his army friend.

When Rusty saw the bushes rustle on the other side of the clearing just outside the fence, he knew it was the Sioux warrior. He would be returning for his horse. He probably intended to finish off what he had started. Rusty weighed in his mind if he should interfere or not. He didn't want to shame the captain any more than he had already been. He decided to wait rather than shoot the Indian as soon as he showed himself and save them a possible problem. This time it wasn't going to be a friendly contest. If it happened as he believed it would—it was going to be a fight to the death.

"Here he comes," Angus said. He had a knack for stating the obvious.

The Sioux warrior no longer tried to hide but made a show of how he pranced into the compound on his muscular mustang. The horse reared, and they both showed their fierceness. Today the warrior was painted for war, as was his horse. Now there was no mistaking his intentions.

Levi and the captain stopped at the edge of the clearing. Both mules behind them protested. They could smell their stables and wanted to be unloaded and set free in their corral. The other horses whinnied and neighed. The young mountain man glanced over at Rusty, who sat with a rifle across his lap. He shot the captain a questioning look.

"Whatcha wanna do, Captain?" Levi asked. They all knew what was to happen next.

"Stay out of this, Levi," the captain said. "This is between that Sioux brave and me. I reckon I shouldn't have bested him in front of all his friends. I obviously have a lot to learn about Indians, don't I? Up till now, every decision I've made seems to have been wrong. This is something that I unwittingly brought on myself, and I plan to settle it myself. If he wins, let him leave—don't kill him. We have enough revenge on our consciousness as it is. At least it'll be as fair a fight as can be. We've already been through the steps."

"I don't know if you're too danged brave for your own good, or is it you're just too hardheaded?" Levi spat. "You and me are as different as night and day. How in the world did we become friends?" Levi Johnson smiled, nodded, and added, "However you want it, Captain Forrester."

Levi spat a stream of brown juice into the dirt and grabbed the lead of the mules. He gave his friend a stern look and shook his head in resignation.

"You best go get your horse if'n this is whatcha want," Levi said. "I reckon we could run him off, but he'd only come back to finish what he started. Now he's gonna die for his desire for revenge. It makes no sense, but that's how it is."

"The first time, it was a close call," Captain Blade said. "I might not be so lucky when the pressure of danger is added to the formula. Like I said, if he wins, let him go. There's no need for more bloodshed."

Forrester turned on his heels and ran for the stables. Nobody said a word. Rusty moved his eyes from the Sioux Indian to Levi. The young mountain man shrugged his shoulders, pointed to his gun, and shook his head. Rusty nodded; he understood, and he stood down. This second contest was between Black Bear and the captain, but it would be for keeps this time.

When Bill came prancing up on his stallion, his face was an expressionless chiseled mask. He only had eyes for the warrior in front of him. He drew his long sword from its sheath. Bright rays of sun reflected off the polished steel.

The Sioux warrior's tomahawk hung from a leather tie around his wrist as he clutched the handle in his white-knuckled fist. The flat black stone was razor sharp. The warrior's eyes were like black chunks of coal. His mustang stomped the ground in anticipation.

Today there would be no starter nor any referee. It would be a personal fight between two men. It would be a battle about honor and nothing more. For these two, there were not spectators today. Only witnesses to what was about to happen.

Nobody said a word. Nobody spoke Sioux except for a few words known by Rusty, but he wasn't getting involved in this. He knew whatever he did, he could end up mixed up in something he didn't want to have anything to do with. He had had enough trouble with Sioux warriors in the last decade. They often saw the white men as enemies, and since he had no plans on moving, he stayed out of fights with other Indian tribes whenever he could manage.

Angus was married to an Indian, so he understood better than any of them what this meant to the Sioux warrior. They believed heavily in their spirit world, and he wished to pass to the other side with honor and not in disgrace as he was right now. He was willing to give his life to retain that honor.

The Indian on the mustang bravely rode into the white man's compound. He feared no one. He already knew he was to die here. At least he planned to die with honor. When the captain brought his white stallion into the compound, he found himself on the farthest side of the fence. The opponents' eyes locked.

The Sioux moved his flat hand across his forehead—the sign of a pony soldier. Then he put his fist to his heart, moved his hand to push it away, and pointed to the captain. In sign language, he said the captain was evil—his enemy. The time had finally come for the reckoning. The warrior seemed very confident, but it was hard to tell with the captain. He had already gone to that place soldiers go to when they have to wreak the wrath.

The nervousness dropped away with the anxiety of waiting. There would be no more waiting as the clash was near at hand. Both men stared at each other with stone faces, but their horses betrayed their true feelings. They both stomped the ground, ready to lunge forward and attack. This was how both animals were trained. Now it was time to discover who was really the better between the captain and Black Bear the warrior.

As Levi watched, beads of sweat stung his eyes, but he never blinked. He knew when it came, it would be fast and furious. Either man could lose their life in the blink of an eye. The two men on the porch, too, had their eyes trained on the white and red warriors.

When Forrester slapped his horse's rump with the flat of his sword, it leaped into a charge. The animal's nostrils flared as he sped toward the enemy. A war cry escaped the Sioux's lips, and his horse jumped into action and roared toward the stallion.

Everything seemed to have shifted into slow motion. At least for the men at odds with each other. For the spectators, it happened in the blink of an eye. The captain saw the warrior draw back his primitive hatchet as his muscles ripped across his body. He glistened with bear fat. That was his only mistake.

When the horses came head-to-head, both men had their weapons poised, and they seemed to swing their blades simultaneously. As the mustang reached the captain, the men on the porch saw the Indian's head tumble off its body and roll across the compound. At the same instant, Black Bear missed his mark but still lobbed off the captain's arm. The sword fell into the dirt as he grasped it with two hands. Bill stared at his newly acquired stump as blood squirted out with each beat of his heart. He turned his head to confirm the Sioux warrior's death. Then he passed out and fell to the ground.

Levi ran for all he was worth to his gravely injured friend. He was bleeding to death. He had both won and lost the fight with the Sioux. The Indian had lost his life but regained his honor. He had faced the white devil and made him suffer the consequences. The captain would remember this moment for the rest of his life—if he survived. Now, the Indian could pass over into the spirit world in peace.

When Blade came around and the pain hit him, he bit his tongue until it bled, and claret freely ran down his chin. Rusty rushed up and gave him a thick piece of leather to bite on to fight against the pain and keep from swallowing his tongue.

Levi was already using pigging string and a stick to tighten a tourniquet around his bleeding stump. Angus ran into the house, grabbed a shovel, and scooped hot coals from the breakfast fire. They knew they had to be quick. Rusty already had one of the tin buckets they had bought at the trading post, and Angus dumped the burning cinders inside.

Captain Blade bit down hard on the thick piece of leather, and Levi grabbed his stump and shoved it into the coals. Forrester's muffled screams came from someplace deep inside. Then he passed out again. The smell of burning skin made Levi retch.

"As soon as my wife, Pine Leaf, gets here, she'll use some of the tribal remedies to help avoid a fever," Angus said.

"Did you see the way those two went at each other?" Levi asked. "It's a miracle the captain wasn't killed right off like the Sioux warrior. I doubt I've ever seen such a deadly clash."

"He ain't out of the woods yet," Rusty said. "He's winged bad, and he may not make it. That's something you best get straight in your mind right now."

"Gather that man's head up and let's bury it with the body," Angus said. "I believe the Sioux would look poorly on us if'n we didn't at least put him to rest with his parts intact. I'd rather my wife didn't see the dead Indian. It might make her uneasy with new boys and all."

"She's gonna know something's up as soon as she sees the captain's arm's missing," Rusty said.

"Lord, have mercy," Levi huffed. "That Indian might have killed the captain. Time will tell if his wound gets infected or not. He'll never be the same."

"That he won't," Rusty said. "Not to worry, son. In my time, I've known several men who lost limbs and still became mountain men despite their handicaps. Now he won't be much good as a soldier, that's for sure. If he had second thoughts, I reckon it's too late for that now."

Levi knew the captain had second thoughts. He felt he was so mixed up inside that he didn't know what he wanted to do at this point, especially after losing half his patrol. He nodded his head. He, too, agreed that the captain's future had been decided for him. That is if he lived to recover from his wound and learned to live without his arm. Some men could do it, while others were too proud or vain to accept such a blemish. Others relished in the challenge and overcame their handicap. Time would tell which type of man Capt. Blade Forrester was.

Angus's Crow wife came as soon as they shoveled the last dirt over the dead man's grave at the edge of the forest. When Pine Leaf saw the man with the missing arm and all the blood, she shooed the men away and went to work on the injured. She was the daughter of the tribe's medicine man and had watched her father cure wounded and sick warriors all her life. She knew exactly what to do and wasn't put off by all the blood or the fact that he was a white man, not an Indian. Some medicine men thought it was bad medicine for them to touch a white man. Some were full of evil spirits and could be dangerous.

Pine Leaf didn't feel any danger from the white man who lay unconscious on the cot in the cabin. He quickly became hot to the touch—he already had a fever. She had noticed his young friend, too. The one they called Levi. Time would tell if these two newcomers to the Rocky Mountains would survive or perish like many others before them.

She wondered what it was that made these men live in the wilderness like Indians when they were clearly ill-prepared. There was something unique about the two new men, but she couldn't say precisely what it was. Maybe it was the same thing Rusty saw in Levi.

For days the captain faded in and out of consciousness. His fever peaked the second day, and Pine Leaf thought he wouldn't make it. On the third day, the fever dropped. The herbal medicines Angus's wife used to heal the captain worked. On the fourth day, he was sitting up again. Lucky for him, he'd lost his left arm, and he was right-handed.

After a week, he sat out on the porch with the rest of the mountain men. Levi had been accepted into the fold and was now considered an equal. The grizzly bear he killed was one of the biggest they had seen, and he killed it with a single shot to the eye. He grinned as he listened to the older men tell tall tales and exaggerations all day long. It was Sunday, and they all took off work on the Sabbath when the situation allowed.

"Maybe we're gonna have to find ya another name," Rusty said to the captain. "Somethin' more appropriate for the current situation. Maybe *Stumpy* will be more in order."

Capt. Bill Forrester shot a glance at Rusty that would peel the paint off a wall.

"Lighten up there, son," Rusty said and chuckled. "If you take what happened to heart, you're just making your life miserable. Maybe you should have a name that doesn't bring the feistiness out in the Indians. Blade is a right challenging name."

"Why don't we just call 'im Bill until something else comes to mind?" Levi grinned. "I wouldn't like to be called Stumpy either. We got to be able to come up with something in between. I agree it shouldn't be the name of a warrior. I reckon that part of your life is behind ya, Captain, and I'd say it's for the best."

The realization that the soldier would never see military life again seemed to sting. Even though he had decided to ride north rather than return to humiliation, he never stopped feeling like he was an army captain. Now that he thought back on the Sioux warrior, he saw it was a similar situation to his with the army back at Fort Leavenworth. Both men had been humiliated. The Indians dealt with the situation with more honor.

He had lost his pride on the trail from Wichita and his arm in the Rocky Mountains. He wondered what he was going to lose next. Probably his life if he didn't learn to adapt like Levi had. Then again, Levi was sort of a mountain man when he lived back in Indiana. He had always been an outdoorsman. As dim as things looked, he still had his life thanks to Pine Leaf, Angus's Crow wife.

They sat on the porch and watched the sky turn into a fiery red as the sun disappeared behind the jagged mountains. The temperature dropped as soon as the canvas of stars rolled across the sky. The men and Pine Leaf all covered themselves in bearskin coats.

They all looked up at the sky until their necks ached as a shower of falling stars raced toward earth, only to burn up before their arrival. When the moon rose shortly after, it was so big it looked like a giant pumpkin and appeared so close, Levi reached out to touch it and see if it was real.

27687269R00049